W9-BDQ-748

A COMPLETE LISTING

OF

THE WORKS OF

ROBERT NATHAN

WILL BE FOUND AT THE END

OF THIS VOLUME

THE WILDERNESS-STONE

THE WILDERNESS-STONE

BY

ROBERT NATHAN

New York
ALFRED·A·KNOPF
1961

Acknowledgment for brief passages of poetry included in this novel is made to:

A FEW FIGS FROM THISTLES by *Edna St. Vincent Millay*, published by Harper and Brothers, by permission of Mrs. Norma Millay Ellis. Copyright 1922 by Edna St. Vincent Millay, Copyright renewed 1950 by Edna St. Vincent Millay.

JOHN BROWN'S BODY by *Stephen Vincent Benét*, published by Rinehart & Company, Inc., by permission of Brandt & Brandt. Copyright 1928 by Stephen Vincent Benét, Copyright renewed 1956 by Rosemary Carr Benét.

COLLECTED POEMS OF ELINOR WYLIE, by permission of Alfred A. Knopf, Inc. Copyright 1921, 1932 by Alfred A. Knopf, Inc., Copyright renewed 1949 by William Rose Benét, 1960, by Edwina C. Rubenstein.

THE GREEN LEAF: THE COLLECTED POEMS OF ROBERT NATHAN, by permission of Alfred A. Knopf, Inc. Copyright 1931, 1935, 1950 by Robert Nathan.

L. C. catalog card number: 60–53444

THIS IS A BORZOI BOOK,
PUBLISHED BY ALFRED A. KNOPF, INC.

Copyright © 1961 by Robert Nathan. All rights reserved. No part of this book may be reproduced in any form without permission in writing from the publisher, except by a reviewer who may quote brief passages in a review to be printed in a magazine or newspaper. Manufactured in the United States of America. Published simultaneously in Canada by McClelland & Stewart, Ltd.

FIRST EDITION

TO ALL MY FRIENDS *herein remembered*

(not always accurately),

the loving dedication

of this book

THE WILDERNESS-STONE

CHAPTER 1

Each generation sees and hears a different world.
I do not live within sound of the great forests, the
primeval wastes in which my ancestors lived. I cannot hear the sound even in my mind's ear. I can
only just remember, faint and far away, the sound
of gaslight and cobblestones. But am I any further
from the one than from the other? The past is

equally far away, wherever it is: today already begins to recede, it fades away behind me—while tomorrow eludes me completely, who was brought up on "The Star-Spangled Banner" and the works of Henry Wadsworth Longfellow.

But spring is always the same. It was no different three years ago when Miranda and her daughter came to live in the apartment next to mine, on Fountain Avenue. I keep half expecting to see her every time I turn the corner, but that is all over, she will never come back here again. Should I even recognize her if she did? It is unlikely. She would scarcely be the same girl I remember—slender, young as a spring morning, with elm-colored hair and thrush-brown eyes.

And Bee; would he still be the way I remember him, if he had lived?

It is spring now, in the year 1960; and the elm tree buds are beginning to break into leaf. The mock orange makes a sweet smell in the air, and roses are blooming and blossoming everywhere.

From the gardens in the richer part of the city comes an odor of fresh green grass and wet earth; and farther out, along the hills, the air is filled with the fragrance of sweet grass, like Indian baskets.

My apartment faces south: I have a view of the city below me. Far off, across the tiny streets and boulevards, the planes come in and go out at the airport, floating upwards and downwards in slow motion like enormous grasshoppers. I watch them, thinking that she might be on one of them; and knowing that she couldn't be. At night the lights shine out across the city like fireworks, blue, green, red, and gold; she used to come into my apartment sometimes just to look at them. Her own windows faced north and the mountains.

I've always liked to write with the sun on my face; I relax, my thoughts slowly unfold. For the last few years I have been working on my autobiography. But today my thoughts lie curled up like winter buds; if they open at all, it is slowly and uncertainly. What happens to a man?

It is easy to say that life is a radiance rushing away from him in the darkness, growing fainter and fainter; the way a town goes by a traveler in a train at night, first the few scattered lights here and there, and then the streets and the houses, the lighted windows, the yellow street lamps, the neon signs, and then the few scattered lights again and the darkness. But the town is still there behind him, sending its small rosy glow into the sky.

My youth, too, cast its little glow; but that was almost thirty years ago. Is it still there, somewhere, behind me—still fresh and sweet and eager, still shining with its own light in the darkness of time? And is that where Miranda went? To be with Bee?

Bee: B. for Benjamin. We were young together —in his own New England, in New York, in the Village. He was blue-eyed and honey-haired, and like a bright spring morning, gentle and kind and full of fun. He was thirty-eight when he died. I used to read some of his nonsense stories to Miranda's daughter, Abbie, sitting on my balcony in the warm April weather. There was one story in particular, about a household bug with seven squirly legs, who kept insisting that he be treated with more consideration. "After all," he kept saying in a sad, hopeless, eager way, "I'm not just an ordinary bug; I have seven legs, all of them squirly."

And each time when I got to that part of the story, Abbie's little square-shaped face would take on a serious expression, and she would begin to count on her fingers. She could never decide what the seventh leg was for. "Maybe he used it to hold his spoon," I said.

She gave me a scornful look. "Bugs don't eat with spoons," she said.

She was a very practical child; she saw life as it was, under her nose. The first year that I knew her, I used to read to her; later, she read to me. In her thin, reedy voice, tasting every word, she read me pages from the books that she enjoyed. They were not at all like the books of my own childhood, and not at all like Bee's stories: for the most part they were books about how to do things. How to Set a Table, How to Build a Chicken Coop, How to Make a Bed. Once when I asked her if she would like me to tell her a story about a sea-witch, she looked at me blankly. "Witches don't live in the sea," she said.

And she named me several kinds of fish, including the minnow, and the tuna-in-cans. "It's very important for a girl to know about how to do things," she said. "In case she gets married, and has a family."

Already, at that time, she had picked out a husband for herself. His name was Mortimer Fenn, and he was in her class at school. When I asked her what Mr. Fenn intended to do with himself when he grew up, she shrugged her shoulders. A husband was only expected to do manly things, like fishing, or killing spiders, or looking for things under the bed—tigers, perhaps, or lost buttons. How to set a table, how to build a chicken coop, were for the ladies.

"He's only seven," she explained.

Still, Mortimer at seven could tell a Falcon from a Corsair and spot an F-104 at thirty thousand feet. When I was his age I could distinguish between a Simplex and a Panhard, but the difference was noticeable. Today everything looks alike, and everyone wants to resemble his neighbor as much as possible. As a result, nobody stands out, except a few old men left over from handsomer times.

In this clutter and lack of singularity, I must place my nephew, Claude.

Claude works for a real-estate company; among his duties is the broadcasting of their commercials over the local television stations. He is a good-looking young man, but not a happy one; he has the look of his generation, which has grown up both uneasy, and indignant at the world. He feels that his future, as well as that of mankind, has been placed in jeopardy because of the bomb, and that the population explosion is creating unusual business opportunities. In this he is not alone; like so many people nowadays, he is in the uncomfortable position of having to believe in the rising value of property and the necessity for expansion and insurance, while convinced that the world could end at any moment. It is a curious dichotomy.

I cannot say that Claude and I were ever very close; but after Miranda Jostyn moved into the apartment across the hall from mine, I began to see more of him. She had few if any friends in the city; she was grateful to him for his attention, and it wasn't long before they were "dating." There was nothing serious about it—not at first, anyway; like Claude, Miranda found the future dark. The only difference was that she was not afraid to look back to the past.

Not that she had, herself, many happy memories to look back to; she preferred to listen, or to read, to let other people look back for her. From the very beginning, I knew that she enjoyed being with me at least as much as she enjoyed being with Claude; and as we got to know each other better, she began to tell me about herself.

She was an only child—"Like Abbie," she said cheerfully, "which makes her the only child of an only child. But I certainly wasn't spoiled; and neither is she."

As a matter of fact, she had been Abbie's age when the war began—the Second World War; and her marriage some ten years later ended in divorce. She'd like to marry again, she thought—some day, but this time for love, with which she had had very little experience. "I read about it in books," she said, "and I don't know what they mean. It was never that way for me—not with Jostyn, or anybody."

She rarely thought about her ex-husband; if she had any feelings about him at all, they were of mild pity, and regret. "I didn't know," she said, "and he couldn't tell me. I guess it wasn't that way with him, either."

She had a small income, not quite large enough, and no way of adding to it, but she was able to pay her rent, and even entertain in a modest way.

"After all," she said, "I'm used to small ways." She could never remember when she'd had enough of anything—of friends, of clothes, or even a home. "Like when we moved from Indiana," she said; "the van wasn't big enough, and I had to leave my rocking chair behind. It wasn't a very good chair, it was sort of coming apart, but I missed it."

Something was always going wrong; the van wasn't big enough, or the roof would leak, or her father would lose his job and they'd have to move again. . . . "That's the way it was," she said. "There was always the sword of what's-his-name hanging over us."

She laughed cheerlessly. "And now it's hanging over the whole world," she said.

I thought of how it used to be when Bee and I were young—when we were Miranda's age. What a shining thing life was then, full of enormous joys and sorrows, the vague, beautiful sorrows that were bigger than the heart; and pity for the world, and for ourselves with less reason.

One day I was sitting with Miranda on the balcony of my apartment in the mild winter weather, watching Abbie and Mortimer playing on the terrace below. It was well on in the second year of Claude and Miranda's going together, and Claude had not yet declared himself in any way. I thought it strange, and so—I think—did she; but then, we fell in love differently when I was young. "You were born in the wrong time of the world, Miranda," I said. "You were born in the wrong season."

I remember that day because it was the first time that Miranda ever talked about Bee; the first time, that is, that his name seemed to mean more to her than simply another of my friends . . . old men and moss-covered women who lived long ago.

"Tell me, Edward," she said matter-of-factly, "would I have liked it in the old days? The way it used to be?"

"Yes," I said. "Almost surely."

"It's like history," she said; "it's all so far away.

And it's so strange to think that you were a part of it. It's like talking to Cromwell, or George Washington."

"Thank you," I said dryly. "You forgot Tiberius. And Leonardo."

She leaned forward in her chair, a curiously intent expression on her face. "Tell me about your friend," she said. "The one you call Bee. The one who wrote the stories you tell Abbie."

"He was a poet," I said. "And he died young." And I felt a kind of sorrow for it, although it was so long ago.

She seemed surprised to hear that he was dead. "What a pity," she said. "What a dreadful waste."

"All the more," I said bitterly, "because he felt so much delight. Being with him was like being drunk with joy. Perhaps I only remember it that way—or perhaps it was only because we were young. But my memories are all of beauty, and laughter."

It seemed a strange combination to her, and she said so.

"Beauty goes very well with laughter," I said, "and best with delight. There were many days, and many moments; but those are the ones that I remember."

I told her how Bee and I had walked all night in the city, talking about heaven and earth and time and eternity, and how we had watched the dawn come up, sitting on the curb with our feet in the gutter, and the tops of the high buildings like golden lozenges in the light. It was in the spring, I told her, and the moon was going down in the west in the blue-dusty sky. The street where we sat was still in cold shadow, but in the north and in the east the sky was already rosy, and overhead it was a clear green, like a melon. The street lamps went off, and a few windows lighted up high in the air across the Park. The city was awake, it breathed gently around us; one sea-going hack with its slumbering horse still stood wearily in front of the fountain in the Plaza. It was so beautiful and breathless; nothing moved, the whole world stood at tiptoe, waiting, and our souls rose up, and we sat there with our feet in the gutter.

"I remember how we rode downtown on the top of a bus," I said, "and ate potatoes for breakfast."

"Why potatoes?" asked Miranda.

"They were there," I said simply, "and they happened to be all we had at the time. As a matter of fact, there was a whole winter when I lived on almost nothing else; but it scarcely mattered. I was writing my first novel; and besides, I was in love."

I told her how I lived in those days in a tiny room on Twelfth Street, hardly big enough for my desk and an old upright piano, and slept and cooked my potatoes in the bathroom. I can still remember the dry and dusty smell of that old house. Bee had a big, bare loft over a paint store; but he had an uncle and aunt uptown to whom he used to go for dinner every week, and sometimes he took me along. I thought that the girl I was in love with that year was the most beautiful woman in the world, and every morning I woke up with a feeling that the world was all full of wonderful things. I expected my book to make a fortune.

"Did it?" asked Miranda curiously.

"No," I said.

"There weren't any wonderful things when I was little," she said; "at least, I don't remember any. We moved a lot, I think, from one place to another. I had mostly made-up friends: a make-believe snake, a butterfly that knew me, and two little boys named Nifty Biddy and Nosey Robinson. Anyway, that's what they were called. I played with them sometimes; I used to bake them mud pies in Ohio."

She gazed down at her daughter who was describing to Mortimer Fenn the world as it appeared to her. I didn't know what she was telling him, but Mortimer seemed resigned to the facts. "She never baked a mud pie in her life," said Miranda. "She uses Quick-Mix. Her cooking isn't very good, but I suppose that in a year or so . . ."

She sighed. "Nobody's a child any more," she said.

It's true, I thought: they marry early now, and have children of their own. It's a very solemn business. Still—the Elizabethans . . .

"They weren't real either," said Miranda sadly. "The two little boys."

"They had marvelous names," I said.

"I gave them their names." She shook her head in a puzzled way. "And yet," she said, "I can't imagine sitting in the gutter watching the dawn come up. With anyone. Can you? With Claude, I mean?"

"Well," I said cautiously, "he might enjoy it."

She gave me a helpless look. "He'd be thinking about Russia," she said. "Or some new development."

"We had our worries, too."

"Yes," she said. "But you didn't have anything to be afraid of; not really."

"Only death," I admitted.

She waved it away impatiently. "Oh, that," she

said; "just anyone's death . . . that isn't what worries us. It's the end of everything; of man himself;
that's what's so awful."

"I suppose we didn't think about it," I said, "because we didn't have to. We always expected it to
go on forever."

"Well," said Miranda, "you can't sit in the gutter
at midnight and talk about the end of the world.

"Sometimes I think if I were old, I wouldn't
mind so much. . . ."

She looked away in sudden embarrassment, and
blushed, but she needn't have. I make no excuses
for my age; it was honestly arrived at. "If the world
is really going to end," I said, "I'd rather be young
and in love."

She said nothing for a moment; then she turned
and looked at me gravely. "You always were,
weren't you?" she said. It was more a statement
than a question, and I didn't challenge it.

"Was that the way it was with everyone?"

She seemed altogether serious, as though she was
trying to understand something outside her ex-

perience. "Well," I said lightly, "it wasn't a move-ment, if that's what you mean. Like the lemmings' march to the sea. It was just that the whole world was at spring. . . ."

She sat still, lost in thought. "I guess I've never had anything like that," she said at last. "There's never been that wonderful sudden morning when all the flowers smell and the birds sing."

"If I were only thirty years younger—" I said, and left it there. Let's not be too much the elderly gallant, I told myself. But I felt, for a moment, the way an old war horse might feel, hearing the trum-pet sound from far away. "Hrmmm," I said. "Ah, well."

She was looking up at the sky, that blue wide pale sky of California over the red roofs and the white city, with the burning somewhere behind the blue. "I suppose your friend Bee was in love, too," she said in a small voice, "with the second most beautiful girl in the world?"

I don't know what it was that gave me the kind

of feeling you get when you run into something in the dark. Perhaps it was the way she said it—not so much a question as a statement, as though she already knew the answer; perhaps it was realizing that she hadn't been thinking about me at all. I took a moment or two to answer.

"He was in love with a married woman," I said at last, "but she was away that year, and I never met her."

CHAPTER 2

It is all mystery, without and within; we are surrounded by mystery. The galaxies peer down on us from the black outer sky, their thunderous roaring reduced to silence by space and time; within my breast my heart steps quietly forward, *tok, tok,* step, step, into the wilderness. All our tomorrows and our yesterdays lie stretched around us like a pattern of fields and hollows, under the same sun. Fly over them and see!

It is all very well to say "fly over them," but to Claude no such flight is possible. One must have imagination to make a journey of that sort, one must believe that the past was not altogether without beauty or purpose.

Claude lumps me in with Queen Victoria, Fisk, and J. P. Morgan; I belong to the world of the Habsburgs. "It's always the old men," he said, "who let the world slide into war, and then blow it sky-high. Next time the pieces won't come down again."

"And yet," I said mildly, "all about me young men and women are marrying and raising large families of children, which seems to me very optimistic, considering what is in view."

"They aren't wasting any time," said Claude. "They're in a hurry."

"And you?" I asked; "and Miranda? Are you also in a hurry?"

"We're dating," said Claude.

He seemed satisfied with the situation, whatever it was. Apparently he wasn't in any hurry himself.

Still—how many young people today enjoy the grand passions, the exquisite anguish or the soaring raptures which my own generation experienced, and even sought? There is an orderliness to the relations of the sexes nowadays, a comfortable acceptance of the facts of life: the boys and girls, the young men and women conform to the rules which are like those for a solemn and delicate dance, a saraband or a minuet. It is all quite placid, and commonplace, and sometimes brutal, and reminds me of the insects who also accept the facts of life without sentimentality.

"Neither of us," said Claude carefully, "is dating anybody else."

I wondered if Miranda was equally satisfied; and if she, too, was not in a hurry. "What I can't understand," she said to me, "is how you could have been so happy. It was as if you had all the time in the world to be young in."

"But we did have," I said, "or we thought we did. It was a long, long springtime, and goodness and love were going to make the world over. Another thousand years—or the day after tomorrow . . . or the next election. There was plenty of time."

"And now there isn't any time at all," she said; "the whole end is only fifteen minutes away, if they come in over the pole. The end of everything; mud pies and Indians."

"And apple pies," I said, "and music. It's unlikely that anyone will ever again go to afternoon teas, or speak English or Japanese, or study the zither."

She shivered suddenly as though she were cold. "I know," she said faintly; "but don't. . . ."

She gave herself a shake. "Claude thinks it's only a matter of a few years," she said matter-of-factly, "before the Chinese have the bomb, and then— Whoom! for everybody."

She sat there, staring out at nothing in particular, and looking solemn. "I wish I were a scholar," she said at last. "I wish I could be soaked in history, like a dumpling. Then I'd choose my own best time in the world."

"There weren't many, for a woman," I said.

"But your time," she said; "the one you've been telling me about . . . That was a good time, wasn't it?"

"Yes," I said. "That was a good time."

I thought about how it had been: the boys and girls, the young men and the young women, fresh out of college, or in from the Middle West, full of dreams and anger, full of eagerness, looking for love and fame, looking for life, on fire for beauty . . . for the first time free, meeting, mingling, searching. . . .

"Of course," I said, "we were drunk often, and we had some famous suicides. In some ways, the times were villainous; not everyone was happy. But people didn't give up easily in those days. I remember a book in which someone said: 'Even for us who have nothing, the day is full of hope, at least until mid-afternoon.' Well, you can see there was a certain eagerness there. . . .

"What we wanted was the right to love."

"I just wanted to be friends," said Miranda.

I could imagine that friends were hard to find in the war years when Miranda was little. And afterwards there was dating and going-steady, and the need to be like everybody else, that drive to conform, to escape from singularity . . . it was all very different from our own time of being young.

And now Abbie was already preparing for marriage at the age of eight, turning her back on fairy tales, and studying the How-to books, all the details and duties of womanhood, including the building of chicken coops.

We went sometimes to picnic by the sea, the three of us, or occasionally four, when Abbie invited her friend Mortimer to come along. He was a sandy-haired little boy, given to sudden fits of running and leaping about, followed by solemn silences, in which he seemed to drink in the world about him with all its wonders, none of which amazed him.

On the sand, Miranda and I settled down on a

large green blanket, under a striped umbrella, while Abbie immediately set to work on a house built of sand, kelp, and a few pieces of wood. But Mortimer ran up and down the beach as fast as he could go. "I'm a Maserati," he said. "I'm a Sebring Special."

"Well, stop being it," said Abbie, "and pay attention to your family of seven children."

"I don't want to," said Mortimer.

"We'll play market," said Abbie. "You can be the butcher, and I'll come in and buy eleven pounds of steak."

"All right," said Mortimer indifferently. "How much do you want?"

"I guess what I want," said Abbie, "is what do you think would be enough for seven children?"

But Mortimer was off again, down the beach. "I'm a Thunderbird," he announced.

For lunch we had peanut-butter sandwiches and hard-boiled eggs, milk, beer, salami, and sour pickles. "My mother says for me not to eat any more sour pickles," said Mortimer. "The last time I got home I threw up."

"That was because you ate all the peanut butter," said Abbie.

"I threw up pickles mostly," said Mortimer.

"Please," said Miranda faintly, "let's just be quiet and look at the view."

It wasn't really much of a view where we were, the flat Pacific glittering in the sun, and very little else. The bluffs rose up steeply behind us, bare and brown, streaked with silver-grey; and the waves rose up out of the shallows and fell with a crash on the black rocks and the grey-brown sand. It wasn't at all like the Atlantic, the wind-skimmed blue with its strange clear currents of green, sun-warmed and shadow-swept. I thought of Bee's house at Cohasset, the old large wooden house smelling of flowers and the sea, and the little tidal river that came chuckling in beside it and went singing out again, narrow and swift and cold and green as ice, and how I used to hear it there when

I woke in the morning, in the bright morning of the world, and went out with Bee to lie in the sun on the rocks and the sand.

And the soft summer nights, with the smell of honeysuckle and wild roses . . .

> *"And the shadows move,"* Bee had written,
>   *"and are still again,*
>   *And now even the waves make no sound,*
>   *For the tide has turned in the river,*
>   *And the water is silent."*

"It sounds old-fashioned now," I said to Miranda, "but it seemed beautiful then. There were better poets, of course; we were in college with Estlin Cummings."

"I like Millay," said Miranda. " 'My candle burns at both ends, It will not last the night.' "

I found it hard to think of Miranda burning so prodigally, and told her so. She didn't say anything for a while, and when she did, she changed the subject. "I've promised to take Abbie to Disneyland," she said, "or anyway, to let her take me. Do you think you'd like to go, too?" And then, before I could answer, she said suddenly, "The place I want to go to is Rome.

"Italy," she added, as an afterthought.

"Have you ever been to Europe, Edward?"

I thought of coming down the Alpine passes into Lombardy, beside the grey, rushing, icy rivers, coming down from the Tuscan hills and feeling that long-breathed, sun-warmed quiet, the peace of ancient stones, smelling the cold, damp, moss-and-wine smell of the old towns, seeing the cypress dark against the sky, hearing the church bells everywhere, smelling the dust-and-donkey smell. . . .

"I've been as far south as Siena," I said. "I was in Florence mostly."

She nodded her head; she had no idea where Siena was, and didn't ask me why I hadn't gone any further. "I've never been anywhere at all," she said.

"But your parents," I reminded her: "you told

me that they kept moving from one place to another."

"Oh, that!" she exclaimed. "That was from Ohio to Indiana, to Illinois. . . .

"I've never been to anywhere important," she said, "only little towns. I've never been to New York, or Washington, or places like that. And the thing is, I'm getting old."

"You're not old," I said, smiling. "And you're here, anyway."

"I'm almost thirty," she said with a kind of childish desperation. "Soon it'll be too late."

"When I was your age," I told her, "I thought I was immortal. Except when I had the grippe, of course, or sometimes at night."

"Look, mother," said Abbie: "there's a skin-diver going into the water."

We watched as the strange figure in his diving gear lumbered down to the shore and disappeared in the sea. After a while we saw his head in its diving mask above the waves as he drifted outward beyond the breakers, paddling with his fins.

He is going back to the beginnings, I thought; back to the primordial home, the dark and briny currents from which we came. He is joining the porpoise and the whale, the otter and the seal. He is going back in time.

Not really, of course: the lobster he will prong on his spear is only a far-off descendant of the decapod that scavenged the bottom of the Mesozoic seas. And the waters are colder now. To go back really . . .

I sighed and gazed sidewise at Miranda who sat with her legs curled under her, leaning on her hands and staring at the swimmer's head already small among the waves some distance from the shore. Miranda's elm-colored hair was caught in a light green scarf tied beneath her chin; she looked like any one of the fresh-faced young women waiting on the dock at Woods Hole for the boat from New Bedford. There was something about those Cape Cod girls, long ago . . . a bloom, a joy, a sweet reasonableness. . . .

I sighed again; and reached for a hard-boiled

egg. How little of man's history has been recorded, I thought; even the kings of Akad and Erech belong to modern times. Already, by Abraham, man had been a long while on earth. And in all those millions of years, when was it good to be alive? Only in the few years of my own youth.

Miranda saw me looking at her, and blushed a little. "I was thinking how a person could hide at the bottom of the sea," she admitted, "from all the things that happen."

"I believe," I said, "that my nephew Claude is an excellent skin-diver." And I added, straight-faced,

"There is no hiding place from love down there."

She was obliged to laugh despite herself. "Do you always think of love?" she asked. "I was thinking of innocence."

"There is no innocence at the bottom of the sea," I said, "a fact which is known to any shrimp or minnow. And as for love—in my day it was a thing of great magnificence. So I think about it, and think how today it has become a comfort, like medical insurance, which everyone should have at reasonable rates."

"You must have been a very flowery young man," said Miranda, with a smile. "And as for your friend Bee—he was certainly a sentimentalist."

"He was indeed," I said. "It was a good, lovely thing to be. And when he died, he was as brave about it as anyone."

"You've had enough peanut butter," Abbie said to her friend Mortimer. "Drink your milk."

"I'm a fast diesel," said Mortimer hopefully, eying an escape route up the beach, "on the long grade to Castaic."

"Drink your milk anyway," said Abbie.

Miranda was gazing out to sea again, with her eyes veiled in the shadow of her hand. I heard her draw a long breath; I thought I heard her murmur,

"Magnificence?"

CHAPTER 3

W<small>HEN</small> Miranda invited anyone to dinner, she
picked up all the things that lay on the floor and on
the chairs—the stockings, old magazines, wet
towels—threw them into the bathtub and closed
the shower curtains on them. The effect on the
visitor to her small apartment—particularly in

candlelight—was charming. Abbie's bedroom, on the other hand, was always neat, and a model of order. Once Miranda threw the towels and the magazines into Abbie's room, but Abbie had had a few things to say about it.

Then, with her candles lighted and her martinis made, Miranda would offer her guests a dinner of olives, celery, cold potato soup, deviled eggs, canned asparagus, and little sandwiches cut into squares. They were daintily served, with sprigs of parsley, and followed by fruit and coffee. To Miranda, the most important thing about food was the way it looked.

Sometimes she broiled a small steak or a chop; those were the occasions when Claude was there. I think she meant to make up to him for the way she felt about his courtship; it was her way of saying that she was sorry she didn't feel more deeply about him, but that she respected his size.

It was on such an evening, when both Claude and I were dining with Miranda, that Abbie suddenly burst out of her room and, rushing across the floor in her pajamas which were too big for her, flung herself breathless into her mother's arms. "I had the horridest dream," she gasped, her little face still red and puffy from sleep. "There was this enormous thing, it was a diesel, I guess, or a dinosaur, and I didn't know what to feed it or where to hit it."

"Why did you have to do either?" asked Claude.

She looked at him in surprise. "What would *you* do," she demanded, "if you had a dinosaur?"

"Did it have seven squirly legs?" I asked foolishly, for which I got the contemptuous glance I deserved. "There you go again," she said. "Fairy stories."

It was Miranda who put Abbie back to bed, tucked her in, and gave her a glass of water and some motherly advice. "The best thing to do about a dinosaur," she said, as she kissed the soft, rumpled, hot little cheek, "is just to close your eyes and say 'Go away.'"

"My eyes were closed anyway," said Abbie drowsily. "I was sleeping."

"Dinosaurs lived millions of years ago," said Miranda. "They're all extinct."

"Well, this one wasn't," said Abbie. "He's alive right now."

"Say some magic," said Miranda hopefully; "say 'Whortleberry . . . away!' "

"That's silly," said Abbie, and fell asleep smiling.

Miranda came back into the living room, carrying a tray with three small delicate cups of coffee. "It's funny, the things you dream about," she said. "Diesels I can understand, on account of Mortimer. Like me, dreaming about a moon going down over a city I've never seen. But dinosaurs?"

"Maybe she read about them somewhere," said Claude indifferently, and changed the subject. The nightmares of a child were of no interest to him; presently he was describing the situation in Tokyo as it came in over the wires of the Associated Press. "We are losing out," he said, "everywhere."

I thought to myself, what a way to pursue a woman! One should never try to frighten her with foreign affairs, or with anything other than a good thunderstorm. There is something in the electrically charged air of a storm . . . but no woman gives in to a man because of the end of the world. The frightened civilian, facing Armageddon, gets nowhere.

Yet how strange, I thought: a moon going down over a city she'd never seen . . .

New York; and the two of us, Bee and I, watching the rising dawn . . . She must have remembered my telling her about it. Still, it was a strange dream to have had. Not for me; but for Miranda, stranger than dinosaurs.

"I was up in those hills today," Claude was saying, "doing a live commercial for the Landover people. They have over a hundred lots for sale, from twenty thousand . . . can you believe it? Thirty years ago you could have had the whole thing for taxes. It makes you think, doesn't it?"

There is inflation for you, I thought: the value of land has gone up, but the value of a man has gone down. As Claude said, it was something to think about.

"It's a terrific development," he said. "A great value, actually. Look at the prospectus."

I took the prospectus and glanced at it. They weren't big lots; about room for a house—not too large—and a small yard. The houses—those already built—were the same size, in four models more or less alike, and three colors, and safely restricted. No one would stand out in such a scheme, no one would be either more or less . . . I was sure that Claude would be very happy there. "Yes indeed," I said. "It is a great value."

Outside Miranda's windows which looked to the north, the night-black hills stood up under the night-blue sky, with starlike lights scattered all over them like diamonds on a black velvet tray. What was it they reminded me of? A spilling of fireflies, a scatter of opals? Or the faraway city long ago, towering in the dusk, its windows lighted in the evening sky, and a young man hurrying home across the sheep meadow and the Mall. . . .

I could hear Bee's voice: Do you remember the cool evenings of spring, with the spring odors of the city around us, the grassy smell of New York at night, and the sea-damp and a little odor of wet earth from across the river, or from the Square, and we on our way to the Lafayette or the Brevoort, or maybe Broad's for seafood, and the street lights on, and the sound of hurrying all around us, but in no hurry ourselves, having all the time in the world?

Yes, I said: I remember.

We were all at the Lafayette, in the side room with the black and white marble floor, with the little tables and the chess players. Ray and Coby and Guy and Bee and I, with coffee in front of us on the table, and some red wine in coffee cups, because it was still prohibition. I could hear Coby singing about old Mingolf . . . Ray's song and Guy's: "Mingolf the mighty . . . Hotter than hearths of the herdsmen in winter, Stamped on the tundra . . . In old Lithuania."

"The Lafayette is gone, Bee," I said. "And so is the Brevoort. And Broad's, and the Elevated that made such sharp shadows, and such a clanking thunder."

"Gone?" said Bee; "why, no—it's here, where I am. Like the dinosaur."

"Did you say something, Uncle Edward?" asked Claude.

"No," I said.

Mingolf the Mighty. I could hear the voices, from far away . . . and the sounds of the soft spring night, the motors, the groan of the cable cars, the clop-clop of a horse and carriage, the rumble of the Elevated, the singing . . .

I was in love with a tall, dark-haired, grey-eyed girl that year. And Guy already had his Rackham, later to be his wife; and Bee loved some woman whose name he never told me.

"Edward," Bee was saying to me, "are you all

right?" "Yes," I said, "I'm fine." "I'm thinking of spending the summer in Europe," said Bee. "We could walk like Hannibal over the Alps into Italy." "Ah," I said; "why not?"

Ray got up and went over to talk to Burton Rascoe and Johnny Farrar, and then we all went on to Elinor Wylie's. She was living in University Place then, and being courted by Bill Benét. My own girl was there already (Elinor wasn't quarreling with her for the moment), and the Colums, Padraic and Molly, and E. A. Robinson, standing tall and dark and uncomfortable in front of the fireplace. Elinor had a poem to read us; she'd written it—or rather said it—that morning in the shower. She was like a princess, out of another time, in her gold dress, tall, slender, with her long neck and gold-flecked eyes, and the brown hair curling softly around her face. She was always gentle with me, for some reason. But Bee was like Shelley, which upset her, because she loved Shelley and sometimes confused him with herself.

How clearly the memories came back—the high-ceilinged room, the marble fireplace, the dark gleam of the Georgian breakfront she had brought with her from Washington—the quiet hum of traffic outside, and Elinor's light sweet voice with the little grating crack in it . . . and all tomorrow waiting.

But tomorrow had come and gone, and Elinor and Bill and E. A. Robinson and Guy were gone with it; and Mingolf had been swept aside by the Nazi hordes, and by the Russians. . . . Bee, too, was gone; I had no business listening to him.

"Yes, sir," Claude was saying to the room in general, "there's still money to be made in real estate." I was in California again.

Apparently I hadn't lost more than a moment or two of the conversation. "All you need," he said, "is to find some empty land somewhere in the desert and divide it into lots. You put in a few streets . . . and in ten years there's a city."

"I thought you didn't believe in the future," I said.

Claude looked at me with a brooding expression.

"In any case," he said, "you've got to think about security." His voice trailed off uncertainly. "Like everybody else," he said.

Security, I thought: the catchword of the times, for the young, for the old. To be accepted, and safe, to be of a kind, not alone, not unique . . .

But what security was there against the Last Trump? Except perhaps to turn from the world altogether, into the arms of the Church or the mystics. One needed a vocation for that sort of thing. Of course, the trump might be delayed—at least for a while; then the best thing was to own real estate.

Even to die the same way as everybody else must be a comfort, I thought. There are so many things to fear in the world, and so many reasons not to put oneself forward. Such reasons and fears, and a natural embarrassment, are also to be found in any chicken coop, whose worried inhabitants never seem to want to be first or last, but always second, or in the middle. That way they share the common hope, which is for corn, and the common fate which is—although they don't know it—to end in the soup. As far as the coop can give a feeling of security, it has given it.

Claude gazed somberly out at the dark loom of the hillside under the light night sky. "Give us fifty years," he said, "and we'll have a paradise working for us here on earth. If we're not all dead."

"In fifty years," said Miranda, "Abbie will be fifty-eight. She'd die in the bloom of her middle age."

She laughed, and then gave a sudden helpless little gesture. "Well," she said defiantly, "I mean it! After all . . .

"There's no escape from it, is there? There's no hiding place."

"None that I know of," I said, "in the body of this flesh. But perhaps on another star, or in another time . . ."

"There'd still be tomorrow," said Claude, "no matter where you were."

"Tomorrow," said Miranda slowly. "Yes . . .

"Or yesterday?" she said.

CHAPTER 4

I HAVE thought a great deal lately about imagination, which seems to me to be man's only link to
that reality which we call God, or some of us,
Spirit. Certainly it is nonsense to think that God
could exist in a material sense in a material universe—that is to say, a something eternal and in-
finite, being also, at the same moment, time-bound

and finite, a creature visible, like a man, in three dimensions. So, in those visions of God which men have claimed to have had, they must have transcended their own limitations.

It is not out of the question. Perhaps the angels who destroyed Sodom and Gomorrah came from outer space as Professor Agret suggests; perhaps we shall join them some day among the galactic clouds. It is even possible that other beings, from distant stars, have been here on earth with us; but they were not beings in our sense of the word, and they were not here in our time, but in theirs. Time is a dimension; it is not the same thing for a virus, a May fly, or a star.

Light is not the fastest thing in the universe; something else moves more swiftly yet, beyond space and time, and hurls itself in every direction at once. In less than a second it travels to the moon or to Andromeda, or to the invisible virus hidden in a drop of blood. Imagination is as mysterious as the universe itself, as mysterious as love.

When I speak of imagination, I am not speaking of memory, of those horrors or delicacies put together out of travel books and fears, old tales and dragon's blood, Lucifer, legend, and photographs of the moon. I am talking about something as pure as mathematics or ice water. I believe it to be man's soul, the only thing he has freed of the complaining flesh. Somehow in the universe, somewhere in the imagination, is God; and imagination searches for Him: the soul seeks Him out.

At the same time, there is something to be said for Claude's point of view. In a threatened, gloomy world, one must prepare for the eventualities, either to live, or to die; if to die, there is no use being gay about it, but if one is going to live, one should try to accumulate a bank account or prepare for a pension. The saints and martyrs of the early years of Christianity, expecting the heavens to open at any moment, gave up all thoughts of worldly success; today, nobody is sure.

It could happen at any moment, even by accident. And unlike the awesome but comforting picture of the Apocalypse, heavenly trumpets, and the life hereafter, there is nothing comfortable about the thought of mankind blowing itself to smithereens—and certainly no assurances of immortality, or of surviving the blast, spiritually speaking.

Nevertheless, this generation, with little to hope for, still clings to hope, and on the chance that it may not commit suicide after all, legislates social security for its old age, joins unions, and donates to the Red Cross. Today a lady worker, a Mrs. Cohen, came to see us on behalf of Muscular Dystrophy. When Miranda asked her in and offered her a cup of tea, Mrs. Cohen burst into tears. "I've been up and down the street all day," she said, "and all I've collected is thirteen dollars, five of it from my own husband. People looked out at me from peepholes, as though I was begging, or they said, 'My wife attends to things like that.' Not one of them invited me in, or even asked me to sit down.

"People," she declared firmly, "are rotten. I've half a mind to write to the FBI."

All Miranda could afford to give her was one dollar, and she got a dollar from me. "It isn't the money," said Mrs. Cohen; "it's the good-will.

"And the tea," she added gratefully.

Thinking about it later, it struck me as odd that Mrs. Cohen should expect to find good-will in the world. However, Miranda disagreed with me. "If she didn't think there was good-will somewhere," she said, "she couldn't go on being Mrs. Cohen. She couldn't bear it."

I suppose it is true that hope springs eternal; without it we should have perished in the bear-and-tiger haunted caves of the Aurignacian, long before the sack of Jerusalem. But did our ancestors in those desperate times pity themselves as we do? It seems unlikely.

I believe that there is a popular song of the day, the burden of which is that children of twelve, despite their parents' doubts, are old enough to love. Not, mind you, to vote; but to love. Without going into a twelve-year-old's definition of love, this opens up such vast horizons of irresponsibility that the mind reels. Why twelve? In India it used to be customary for children to be married at the age of six.

The truth is that nowadays everyone wants everything that everybody else has, right away, and without pain. Claude feels that he was born too late, and that he has missed the greatest opportunities.

He speaks, of course, as an American. To an American, the great opportunities are to be found in business, not in love. I tried to explain to him that when I was his age, I knew nothing about business; it seemed to me that everything was as settled as it was ever likely to be. Indeed, we seemed to have arrived at some sort of millennium: the air was full of intoxicating suggestions, it smelled like a spring morning even in winter, everything was happening. Peary had discovered the North Pole, Lindbergh had flown the Atlantic, and Gershwin had composed the *Rhapsody in Blue;*

it was a new world; but my friends and I had no money to invest in it, only our hearts.

Of course, we had our bad times, too. But even in the bad times, in the crash and the Depression, the broken lives, the suicides, the hungry, homeless men and worn-down women, with dust covering the heroes, covering the farms and ranges of the Panhandle, covering the *Rhapsody in Blue*—even then there was something, almost a gaiety, bitter as gall, perhaps, and grim, but brotherly. Not that most people admitted to being their brother's keepers, but along with the anger there was compassion, there was a Steinbeck, there was a Benét.

"There was a something," I once said to Miranda, "whatever it was in us, that loved the world, at least for a while."

"Then that," said Miranda, "is what I missed, and that's what I'm sorry for; for not having that whatever-it-was. Because I can't help loving the world, on a nice day."

"Then have some courage," I said. "Admit that the world is worth loving."

"Admit it to whom?" she asked. "I just did, to you."

It made me stop a minute and wonder. To whom, indeed?

She sighed distractedly. "It's just that I'm in the wrong time," she said. "I should have lived long ago, when you were young."

And she added in a low voice, "Don't think I haven't wished it."

I thought to myself that wishing wouldn't make it so. I shake my head sometimes now, thinking about it.

I was often puzzled by Miranda and her daughter, watching the two of them together. For one thing, Abbie was a sturdy little realist: she had the makings of a matriarch, and I was glad that I had never met her in my younger days, when I would certainly have been her victim. It seemed to me that whatever the destiny of mankind might turn out to be, Abbie would meet it and deal with it successfully; she was already, I thought, preparing for the time when women would take over the earth, or what was left of it—either in the bat-hung caves of the beginning-again, or the fantastic communities of an uninterrupted future.

Toward her mother, Abbie was loving, respectful, and hard as nails; they met, I would have said, on equal ground, but not for long. Given a few more years, Abbie would be telling her mother what to eat for lunch, and not to forget to wear her coat when the weather turned cold. "Mother," she said to me once, "is such a dreamy type. Always moping around and being so sweet and cheerful and everything."

"Well," I said, "you can't be both sweet and mopey, not at the same time, anyway."

"Yes, you can," said Abbie. "You can be mopey on Monday, and the other things on Tuesday. It's all make-believe, anyway."

I asked her what she meant by that. "I mean," she said, "most of the time there isn't anything to be either way about, really. But Mother is always making up things—like what you say to dragons, or things like that."

"When your mother was your age," I said, "she was friends with a make-believe snake, and two little boys named Nifty Biddy and Nosey Robinson."

"That's what I mean," said Abbie. "They weren't real, either."

She glanced at the toy watch on her wrist and made a little face of resignation. "I have Mortimer," she said. And she added simply,

"Mortimer does what I tell him."

"Does he?" I asked. "I thought he was a little restive the other day at the beach."

She gave me a cool glance, but I could see that the word "restive" was new to her. "That's only a phrase he's going through," she declared. I was glad that she was able to make at least that one small mistake.

"I could tell the time," she said, "if I had a watch that went."

"Do you think eight is old enough to have a real

watch," she asked, "that goes?" I said I thought so. "Twelve is old enough to love," she said; "whatever that means."

She thought for a moment, and bent down and scratched her bare, twiglike leg. "If Mother marries Claude," she said, "he'll be my father; and you'll be my uncle." She gave me a childlike look, half grave, half mischievous. "Will you do what I tell you?" she asked.

I replied that I thought it unlikely, and she nodded her head, as though she had expected nothing else. "Old people are hard to control," she said. I had to laugh; she was such a small creature for such a large word. "Do you expect to control Claude?" I asked. "Somebody'd better," she said solemnly.

"Mother's a wisher," she explained. "She's a wishing well. She's not very good at controlling people. She couldn't control my father, but I could."

"How did you manage it?" I asked.

"By screaming," said Abbie.

"Did you love him?" I asked, incautiously.

"I was too little," said Abbie simply. "I just screamed."

Who knows what love is? Nobody is born with it —or with imagination or languages; only with the need to communicate, and the capacity to imagine and to learn. A child learns to talk, and a child learns to love; but a child's love and that of a grown woman are not the same. No matter how much one talks, there has to be someone to listen. My father, who spoke so brilliantly in court, and said everything he had to say to a jury, was never able to communicate his love for me; or perhaps I was never able to listen. Now that I am so much older, I hear more clearly the voices of long ago, while today's young people and tomorrow's children speak to me in tones I scarcely understand.

Miranda, too, heard other voices—how clearly, then, I didn't know, either.

[59]

CHAPTER 5

I REMEMBER the first time I ever felt what it was like to grow old; it was at a performance of *Der Rosenkavalier* at the Opera. Mme Lehmann was singing—that incomparable Marschallin, the eternal woman, wise and sorry, *"ein halb Mal lustig, ein halb Mal traurig."* Shall I ever forget how she sat in her lonely moment on the stage, peering into her mirror, hearing the clock's relentless ticking, and asking herself "How can it be?" that she should grow old . . . she, of all people! *"Wie kann denn das geschehen?"*

To grow old, to leave behind the wind-bright meadows still with their fragrance and their flowers . . . Surely, one should be able to turn, to go back. . . .

Alas, only in memory. Lotte Lehmann will always be singing to Octavian on the stage of the Metropolitan, while I and the woman who was herself the Marschallin to my Octavian lean forward in our seats in the dress circle.

Below us blazed the tiers of glittering boxes, the golden, glowing curtains, the red velvet, the starched shirt-fronts and opera hats, the long, white kid gloves, the powdered bosoms. From the pit there ascended, along with the music, the fragrance of furs, of flowers and perfume.

Afterwards, we sat at the Brevoort over coffee and brioches. "If only we could set the clock back," said my friend with a sigh and lifted her hand, delicate as a lily, to the nape of her neck where her long, brown, shining hair was drawn up in a loose knot. It was a gesture at once delicious, feminine, and self-conscious.

"But then," I said, "we'd not have met."

"It would be still ahead of us," she said.

After a while she remarked: "Tell me; what do you hear from your friend, Bee?"

Perhaps it was the winter night with the dark hard cold outside, and the warm room smelling of coffee and cigarettes . . . or perhaps it was the music singing in my head like summer . . . I felt suddenly sad; so much had already gone by. "He's still abroad," I told her. "In Switzerland, I think."

Her eyes across the table from me grew soft. "You miss him, don't you," she said gently.

"Yes," I said. It was January, in 1936, and although I didn't know it, time was running out.

So memory skips about. Years later, in Hollywood, I wrote the script of a motion picture to include Mme Lehmann and the young dancer Cyd Charisse. Mme Lehmann was to sing, against the fragrant Tahitian night, the melodies of Schubert and Brahms. After I left the studio, the producer had the script rewritten; it ended up as a water-ballet for Esther Williams, and Mr. Howard Keel did the singing; there was no part in it for Mme Lehmann.

But we were friends by then, and we felt badly about it together. It was at that time that she gave me a singing lesson—the only singing lesson I ever had. She sat at one end of her long living room, her eyes hidden behind dark glasses, while I stood at the piano and sang. I think that I sang a song by Hugo Wolf.

After I finished, she said only one thing to me. "Edward," she said gently, "must you look so sad when you sing?"

I received no other teaching; and I cannot say that it taught me anything, except always to look as merry as possible.

But that was much later, and Bee had already been gone a long time.

In those early days we used to discuss the most serious subjects while walking uptown together past the shops with their rich windows in all the colors of the world. But mostly we talked about our love affairs. "Can one love more than once?" Bee wanted to know. "What if I loved some girl a thousand years ago?"

"Why then," I said, "you would be dead these thousand years."

"It seems a shame," he said, "to be limited to what's available."

I told him to be glad that the choice was narrowed down for him. "Think of tomorrow's apple-cheeked girls," I said, "forever young, forever beautiful."

"I think it will be dreary on ahead," said Bee. "I'd rather draw them back to me instead."

"All of them?"

"No," he said slowly. "Only one . . ."

"And then," I said lightly, "what will you talk about?"

He looked at me gravely. "What do the angels talk about?" he said. "Love and forever, without fear of change. Beauty and peace and glory evermore."

"Ah well," I said contentedly, "in that case . . ."

We were happy, walking up the Avenue together. As for myself, I was quite satisfied to be where I was; I might have loved a girl a thousand years ago, but her thoughts and her personal habits would have frightened me. As for the future . . .

Well, that was long ago. Today it is easy enough to be frightened in this apartment facing the sky in which the great jets come and go from every corner of the earth—but in which there are no angels any more.

Instead, there is a sense of malevolence; but I do not think that God has anything to do with it.

No . . . I was only really at home in the world for a little while. It was not simply because I was young; in spite of all the things that were wrong with it, it was, truly, a better world. And when I tell Miranda about it, her eyes fill with longing.

She would like to see something of that world, she would have liked to go with me to Les Halles when the creaking market wagons brought the fresh lettuces, the fruit, the vegetables to Paris in the dark and empty hours before dawn, and we breakfasted on onion soup and wine, and someone played the accordion. Instead, she went off with Claude to look at a real-estate development in Antelope Valley, up through the canyons which are green and sweet at this time of year, and out to the desert which is covered with flowers. The desert flowers are small and they do not last long; sometimes at night when the breeze is from the Mojave we can smell their delicate, shy fragrance. It always makes me think of the Cape in spring, but it was very different there with the shad bush in bloom, and the white foam of the beach plum, and the warm odor of heather and scrub pine and sweet geranium in the sun, and always that good smell of sand and ocean and dried seaweed and dune grass underneath all the other smells.

In her mother's absence, Abbie and I had lunch together at the Farmer's Market. As on every other occasion when we were there together, the captive myna bird whistled at her, which never failed to enchant her; and the aisles between the stalls were packed with people trundling their little market carts behind them. How good everything always looks! The glowing oranges, the fresh asparagus, the fat white cauliflower, the ruby strawberries, the crisp and dewy lettuces; and everywhere there is the smell of burning hickory, of charcoal fires, of meat cooking and new-baked bread. What shall we have for lunch? There is too much, it is impossible to decide between the Mexican kitchen, the Chinese kitchen, the French, the fish-and-chips. . . . I ended up with a salad, and Abbie with a dish of fried shrimps, a hot dog in a bun, a large slice of blueberry pie, two doughnuts, and a chocolate soda. At our feet, tribes and families of little sparrow-like birds flitted about, searching for crumbs and not afraid of anything. People streamed past our table like whole aquariums of fish, all of different shapes and colors; mostly they seemed either very old, or else very young, underfoot, and ready to weep.

We sat, half in the sun, half in the shade of an aluminum umbrella; Abbie made gurgling noises with her straw at the bottom of her glass, a little smudge of yellow mustard at one corner of her mouth, a film of milky chocolate across her upper lip. There was an endless hum and chattering of voices all around us and above our heads. She looked at me with what I thought was a speculative gleam.

"Would you like something else?" I asked. "I'd like it," she replied truthfully, "but I'm about ready to pop."

"You're a sensible girl," I said, thinking of Mortimer, and how strict she'd been with him about the peanut butter; but it is always easier to point the way for someone else. In any case, whether from conscience or the wish to be thought something more exciting than merely sensible, her expression clouded over and for a moment she appeared morose.

"Well," she said at last with a sigh, "somebody has to be."

She looked so solemn—and so gloomy—that I couldn't help smiling. "Do you intend to save mankind all by yourself?" I asked; but she only gazed at me more mournfully than ever. "I'm too little to save anybody," she said.

And she added in a small voice,

"I'm probably going to be sick."

I have no doubt that I looked as alarmed as I felt. "You will have to go by yourself," I said unhappily; "I can't very well go with you to the Ladies'."

"I think maybe if I sit still," said Abbie carefully, "I'll digest."

We sat for a while, until the color came back into her cheeks again, and her expression brightened. "Anyway," she said at last, "now I'll have something to remember."

And she ticked off on her fingers all the different things she had eaten. "You will make yourself ill again," I said. She stopped counting then and took a deep breath. "I know," she said. "But it was such a glory."

She gazed with contempt at a little boy who was fighting with his sister over a paper pinwheel; he had not yet arrived at an age when being a man did him any good. "Children are pretty awful," she said. "I'm glad I'm grown up."

Later, before we left, she made three more remarks. Two of them were questions. "Uncle Edward," she asked, "is Mother coming back today from wherever she went?"

"Certainly," I said. "She will be home for dinner."

Abbie's little face showed neither relief nor

concern. "Tell me something," she said, "did you ever know my father?"

"No," I said.

She sighed a deep sigh, which might have come from having eaten too much. "When I'm really grown up," she said, "I'm never going to let anybody leave me."

Miranda was quiet that evening; she had brought bowls full of yellow poppies home with her; and she had a faraway look and seemed relaxed and contented. She had enjoyed the long drive, she said, the glimpses of the desert and the distant blue-brown mountains, and on the way back, the shadowy canyon where the treetops all but met above the road and the small brooks, soon to be dry, still ran in trickles among the rocks. "Did you behave yourself?" she asked Abbie. "Were you a good girl?" But she scarcely listened when Abbie announced that she had been a very good girl indeed. "A bird whistled at me," said Abbie, "and we saw some puppies and some baskets, and I had a soda and I brought you home an orange." "That's nice," said Miranda vaguely; "I hope you weren't any bother."

"I wasn't," said Abbie. "What did you bring me?"

For a moment, Miranda looked startled; and then she smiled. "I'm not sure," she said. "I don't know yet."

But later, when Abbie was in bed, she came across the hall, carrying a bowl of poppies, and knocked on my door. I brought her in and fixed her something to drink, and made her comfortable in the chair by the fireplace, as it had turned a little cold. "It was a strange day," she said; "I kept forgetting where I was. I mean . . . I knew where I was, but I didn't know when. It might have been long ago. Or it could have been some-body else, and not me at all. It was very restful . . . I wasn't afraid, or worried about anything.

"It was strange," she said. "What do you think it was, Edward?"

I told her that I didn't know. "Perhaps it was the desert," I said. "It does things like that sometimes."

She nodded thoughtfully. "Yes," she said; "perhaps . . . It was like a mirage of some kind. . . ."

She roused herself with a little frown. "I forgot about Abbie," she said. "I forgot to bring her anything. That wasn't very nice of me, was it?"

She looked across at the bowl full of flowers. The poppies were furled for the night.

CHAPTER 6

I'M AFRAID we cannot dismiss God so lightly, simply by saying that there are no angels in the skies any more. If it is true that God is no longer in men's hearts, one must admit that He was never very comfortable there. Yet He is no less present in the universe than in the days when the great cathedrals were being built, and we must find Him or perish.

Bee had no such problems. It never occurred to him to doubt God's presence somewhere, usually near at hand, in a girl's face or a bird's flight or a green-running river. He took God in like sunlight or air, without fear and without any thought of reward or being saved—and without any more love than he might have had for a friend.

I wasn't like Bee at all; I was still a rebel from the theologians, whereas he had simply gone away out of the battle altogether.

I remember one night, looking down from Fiesole at sunset onto the darkening Tuscan plain, with the lights of Florence just coming out like fireflies beneath us, and the church bells ringing across the city. I remember that I felt as though I were back in the medieval world, hearing in those slow-pealing bells the fearful sound of sanctity.

"There," I said, pointing dramatically, "is the world that denied Galileo, and burned Joan of Arc."

"And gave us Leonardo," said Bee gently, "and Fra Angelico."

I probably made an impatient gesture. "There's always a good side," I said, "if you look far enough. You can't make a religion out of that."

"I don't want to make a religion out of anything," said Bee soberly. "The good and the bad change places too fast. The funny thing is that if we'd been alive in 1600, we'd have been happy as kings to be told that Copernicus was an old fool, and that the sun still went around the earth."

And gazing dreamily out over Florence in the deepening dusk, he repeated the first lines of a poem of Elinor's:

> *"Say not of Beauty she is good,*
> *Or aught but beautiful, . . .*

"Let people's hearts rejoice," he said, "for whatever reason. I am probably one of the Chasidim."

"You don't dance," I said, "and you don't embrace poverty. And you're certainly not a Jew."

Bee laughed. "Let's go back to the Villa," he said, "and embrace Josephine."

In those days we were staying in Castello, which is halfway up the hill to Fiesole, in a lovely old villa that had been made over into a private *pension,* set in a Renaissance garden where the nightingales sang all night long. There, between times, Bee and I practised fencing—which was the reason we had come to Florence in the first place, to learn the Italian School. We had joined the Circolo Dilettanti di Scherma in the city, run by the old fencing master, Roberto Raggetti; and there Bee perfected the foil, which had been his weapon at Harvard, and I the saber. The young Italians at the Circolo were gay and friendly; it was still early in the century.

"Avanti! Dirito! Ah-hup!"

There, at one time or another, we saw the two incredible Nadis, Aldo and Beppo, champions of the world, and dreamed of what it would be like to be so swift, so light, so graceful, and so merciless.

After the lessons we used to sit at one of the tables of a small restaurant near the Loggia di Lanzi—or near the Medici Palace, or both, I have forgotten—and with the sun on our faces and the grey medieval walls rising around us, sip our *apéritif*, a white vermouth, very mild and delicate and not too sweet, with a twist of lemon rind in it. Sometimes the American girl, Josephine, came down from the Villa and sat with us there in the mild spring sun.

She was a shy, slender girl, not really pretty, but dainty and feminine; her family for generations had owned one of the great plantations north of Charleston, along the Cooper River. Her eyes took on a dazed and gentle expression when she looked at Bee; she was obviously in love with him, or very nearly, but she retained a certain delicate composure. It wasn't long, however, before she and Bee were disappearing for a little while every evening after dinner; they went, they said, to take the air in the scented, moss-hung gardens of the Villa. It never took young people very long in those days; I myself once walked down Legare Street with a young woman I had met at tea, turned to see the new moon over my left shoulder, and was in love by half past ten. But that was another place and another girl, and this was Bee and Josephine.

On this particular evening, after dinner, at which we had enjoyed a particularly pleasant wine, an Orvieto, pale, cool, and lightly sweet, they excused themselves as usual, and I went upstairs to the room to look over some new books which had arrived from America, among them Elinor's *The Venetian Glass Nephew,* and a long letter from my friends the Benéts: Steve and Rosemary were in Paris, in an apartment on the Rue Jadin near the Parc Monceau, with a Guggenheim Fellowship, a prize cook—*bonne-à-tout-faire* (according to Rosemary) and, as Steve wrote, "the marronier of the tenth of March in bloom."

They sounded happy, grateful and busy. "I have

a nice little room on the sixth floor," Steve wrote, "all swept and garnished. And I am extinguished under the foolscap of a long poem."

I longed to be with them. But it was Bee who was to see them later in Paris, not I.

After a while I went downstairs again to the main hall, and was surprised to find Josephine there alone.

"Where's Bee?" I asked. She gave me a strange look, a little bewildered and at the same time pleading. "I . . . I don't know, exactly," she said. "He was there . . . and then he wasn't. . . ."

She took my hand; her own was cold, and trembled ever so slightly. "Please," she said, drawing me toward the garden. "I want you to come. . . ."

As we walked across the stone terrace in the cool night air, she tried to tell me what had happened—or had seemed to happen. "Because I don't know," she said; "I don't, really. We were sitting on the stone bench by the old statue, the one of Diana I think it is—and we were talking . . . and then suddenly he wasn't there. At least, it seemed as though he wasn't; and yet, he was talking, I heard him. But as though he were far away—and not to me, to somebody else. He was saying the things he'd been saying to me. It was so weird, you see. And I couldn't find him, I couldn't find him anywhere; and all the time I heard him talking."

Her voice shook. "Does it sound awfully silly?" she asked miserably. "You do believe me, don't you?"

The stone bench by the statue of Diana stood cold grey and empty in the tree-hung darkness; there was no one there. Yet, as I stood and stared at it with Josephine's hand in mine, it seemed to me that some encounter of shapes, some meeting of shadows, was nevertheless taking place there before us, an encounter out of time and space, a meeting beyond the hours of the night. "He isn't here," I said stupidly, to which she only whispered: "Can't you hear him?"

I didn't answer, because it was true: I did hear him, it was Bee's voice . . . or did I only think I heard him? . . . in that ghostly garden with its mossy statues glimmering in the starlight, and the heavy scent of garden earth, the meadowy air, the shadowy fragrance . . .

"We have so little time," he was saying; "there is only the space of a grasshopper's song, a bird's note . . . Why you, out of all the world?"

I heard Josephine give a gasp, or a small sigh. "Oh no," she whispered; "please."

But it was another voice, a woman's voice, that answered him. "How young you are," it said. It was a voice I had never heard before, and yet for some reason it seemed familiar to me. "Like a hungry child," it said.

"I am as old as the world," said Bee. "When I was young, the world was full of wonder." "There weren't any wonderful things when I was little," said the voice.

I could hear Bee laugh, or so it seemed. "There is only one wonder," he said: "that we should be here together."

"But where?" cried the voice, "Where are we?"

I didn't hear his reply; it was too much for Josephine, who had been brought up on a plantation among the family ghosts; turning, she fled back to the house, drawing me after her. "Did you hear him?" she kept asking, "Did you? But he wasn't there!"

"I know," I said; and then, wanting to comfort her: "It was some sort of trick; an echo, perhaps."

"Oh, but," she cried, "an echo of what?" I couldn't answer her.

Bee was waiting for us in the main hall when we came in. "Why," he exclaimed, his eyes alight with laughter, "the two of you! And the night so bright with stars!"

But I was vexed at him; so it had been a trick after all. But why? Simply to scare a young girl? Josephine gave him one stupefied glance and rushed up the stairs past him to her room; we heard her slam the door.

"Bee," I said, "Whatever were you up to?"

The laughter suddenly went out of his face. "I wasn't up to anything, Edward," he said. "Anyway—I can't tell you."

"I heard a woman's voice," I said. "I did, didn't I?"

"Yes," he said quietly.

"And it wasn't a trick? You weren't just hiding somewhere?"

"No," he said. "I wasn't hiding."

"But then . . . you were really in the garden," I said, "with someone else?"

"Yes," he said.

But with whom? To whom could he have spoken as he did? *"Why you, out of all the world?"* . . . Something rang suddenly in my mind like a bell. "Was it the one," I asked, "whose name you never tell me?"

He nodded, without speaking.

So that was it! "Well, then," I asked, "did she follow us here to Florence, or have we followed her? At least tell me that!"

I thought that he gave me a strange look, almost of appeal. "Edward," he said slowly, "I don't know."

My disbelief must have shown on my face, for he put out his hand in a helpless gesture. "Truly," he said, "I don't. I cannot tell you."

"But she was here," I insisted. "She was in the garden with you."

"Yes," said Bee. "For a little while."

"Then where is she now?" I demanded. "She can't have gone very far."

"Well," said Bee, "she isn't here."

He stood there with a strange expression on his face, almost as though he were listening for something that no one else would hear. "I'm not sure I know where she is," he said at last. "But I can tell you this:

"It is far away, I think."

CHAPTER 7

My FRIEND Leonard Wibberley has sent me the galleys of his book, *The Quest for Excalibur;* that great bearded laughing furious Irishman has written a novel about knighthood and the dignity of the individual in an age devoted to large social benefits.

Actually, this age of ours is as violent as that of Brian Boru. On every country lane or freeway, gentlemen (and ladies, too, the darling Amazons) encased in steel like King Arthur or the Barons at Runnymede, hurl whole cavalries at one another at speeds of eighty or ninety miles an hour, coming together in holocausts of destruction for no reason at all, or by mistake.

This is not all. In the cities, gangs of young hoodlums armed with knives and tire chains roam the streets, bank robbers flourish, convicts escape, children are abducted, lunatics let out, women ravished, and policemen slain.

Claude takes all such things in stride. But he is indignant at my friend for questioning the advantages of social benefits. "It was the welfare state," he insists, "that brought us through the Depression of the early thirties." He is too young to remember it, but he has a point. Perhaps what I object to is the niggardliness of the comfort which is offered.

Yet the truth is there is too much need and

anguish in the world, and not enough of anything with which to meet it. The balance of nature is a delicate point, for man or beast: you cannot give anything to one portion, without taking something away from another.

Miranda, at least, is not concerned with such matters. I found her reading *John Brown's Body* for the first time; and I remembered how Bee had written from Paris:

"I have been seeing something of the Quincy Porters," he wrote, "and going to the concerts with them, and to the Opera. Our Quincy is in almost violent health and working happily with D'Indy, and our Lois—who, by the way, is prettier than ever—is studying the violin with Maurice Hewitt. They took me to a rehearsal at the Ecole Normale the other day, Cortot and Thibaud preparing the Brahms Double Concerto with an orchestra from the school, and a young American girl, a Miss Wilson, standing in for Casals—if one can "stand in" on the cello. She was quite lovely,

I thought, and played like an angel, and quite young, and comes from—of all places!—Cape Cod; it turned out that we had mutual friends at the Hole. Well, you can imagine . . . and later we all went to a party at somebody's house and met a young sculptor from Texas named McVey, who is over here on a Guggenheim; his money has run out, and he offers to do a head of me and one of Quincy if we'll pay him enough to stay on a few months longer. In bronze, no less. The Porters and Miss W. and Hewitt played a quartet of Beethoven, and I drank a lot of Calvados.

"I ran into Steve and Rosemary Benét the other day, coming in from the Bois; they have a house in Neuilly now, and had been shopping, and Steve, looking like a myopic cherub as usual, had his overcoat pockets stuffed with everything under the sun, cans of sardines, almost the whole of the New York Sunday Times, and the galleys to part of his long poem. He gave it to me to read; it is magnificent. I can't tell you how happy it made me, there is something to our generation after all, it isn't all Fitzgerald. Rosemary looked, as always, like something out of childhood, some good dream, or a wish come true. I have invited them to go with me—and Miss Wilson—to L'Ecrevisse one night next week for dinner, for the écrevisses and the Corton-Charlemagne '15, which is the best in the world; but perhaps they will not, Steve is still feeling the loss of his father, and swore off Montmartre in any case long ago. I may have tea with them instead chez eux, for to admire the new son, and to see Strosephina again. Louis Bromfield is here with Mary, at the best hotel, and Estlin on the Left Bank somewhere, but except for one night at the Dome I haven't seen him. Paris is full of peach-cheeked wonder-eyed American girls with dresses above their knees, dancing the Charleston at all the little boîtes, and English girls all trying to look like Duff.

"Do you hear anything from Josephine? or is she still in Florence at the Villa? I'm afraid I was a disappointment to her, but what is a man to do who is in love with someone outside his life? Perhaps that *someone* will join me here in Paris before the autumn is run out—perhaps I shall never be with her as I would like; we are so little masters of anything.

"What is it Anatole France says? 'A man is master of his own soup, and only when it is in his mouth.'"

I thought it might amuse Miranda, so I fished the letter out of my trunk-for-letters and read it to her. When I had finished, she sat looking at me with an inquiring expression. "What ever did happen to Josephine?" she asked.

"Why," I said, "she went back to Charleston again."

"And the 'someone else'?" she asked. "Did she ever get to Paris?"

She sounded elaborately casual. "I believe so," I said. "She and Bee went for a week to Cadenabbia, on lake Maggiore."

"Cadenabbia is on Como," said Miranda.

After a while, she began quoting from *John Brown's Body:*

> *"I know this girl, she said. . . .*
> *"I know her heart touched with that wilder-*
>   *ness-stone*
> *That turns good money into heaps of leaves*
> *And builds an outcast house of apple-twigs*
> *Beside a stream that never had a name. . . .*

"I like that part," she said. "It's something about the wilderness-stone that makes it seem so real. What was a wilderness-stone, Edward, and why is there something magical about it?"

"We're a stone people," I replied, "on a stone planet. Our first gods were of stone; and our most mystical dream used to be about a stone—the philosopher's stone, which was supposed to turn dross into gold. The wilderness-stone is the dream of freedom."

"If I were free," said Miranda, "I'd be in Cadenabbia."

"In that case," I said lightly, or at least as lightly as I could, "I'm glad you're not, because we'd miss you."

"Would you?" she asked gravely. "Would you miss me if you'd never seen me?"

A moment later she gave a sudden, rippling little laugh. "How do you ever know who's seen you," she asked, "even walking down a street? You're practically invisible most of the time, anyway."

"Not to the people you know," I said; "they see you."

"Yes," she agreed; "but think of all the others— you might as well be in Timbuctoo."

I could feel my heart beating a little faster, as it does sometimes when I catch a glimpse of something I can't quite understand. "Or in a Florentine garden?" I asked, and held my breath. She looked at me without surprise.

"Perhaps," she said simply. "Why not?"

Why not, indeed? Is there anything more difficult to answer than that simple question: why not?

As Pilate said—or didn't say, depending on the sources—what is truth? He was a colonial administrator, and he was not expected to give rein to his imagination. It must have been as unlikely for a Roman procurator in the reign of Tiberius to believe that Jesus was the Son of God, as it would have been for Augustine, four hundred years later, to doubt it. Or for Joan of Arc to doubt her voices—or for Calvin to believe that far out in space, trillions of millions of miles away, other planets revolved around other suns, with other creatures inhabiting them.

One should only believe what one does not know: then one can believe everything, and that is the great comfort.

Claude, on the contrary, gets some sort of comfort out of not believing anything—or in believing only what his contemporaries believe, which is almost the same thing. His favorite remark is: "We have nothing to believe in. All over the world people have nothing to believe in."

This is conformity with a vengeance; and besides, it isn't true.

I think that what Claude and all his generation are feeling is the breakdown of authority in the western world. There is no firm ground any more, neither the Divine Parent nor the human one to whom past generations listened with respect and with a certain trembling. There is no home, such as there used to be; the authority of the father has been whittled away; his word is no longer law, even to his wife. There is no sense of God hovering above the father's chair, or the mother's bed; and without that Awful Presence, the household flies apart, everyone for himself and the devil take the hindmost. Vengeance was always of the Lord; when He hesitated, the head of the house took up the rod. Failing that, one might as well give up.

And of course for the most part we have given up, out of pity for the young, who are so tender and so defenseless, and bruise so easily—a fact which would not have deterred our grandparents for a moment.

Having so little pride in our homes and in our families, we aren't likely to have much pride in our country—unless, like the Russians, we can be proud of hydroelectric installations. Merely to wave a few flags and to dislike someone is not enough.

There is always Abbie to draw me away from such uncomfortable musings.

There are as many faces of love as there are women; no woman has the whole face of love—an eye, perhaps, or the modeling of a nostril, a glance, sound, fragrance, a way of walking. What of a child? It is all there in the hollow bone, the contours and the artifice not yet developed—and the determination to dominate her world by direct assault or by whatever means.

For Abbie, it is the direct assault. She is scornful of the hesitations of her elders; for her, the good conscience is success. "Mortimer!" I heard her cry from down below me on the grass. "Come here."

"What for?" Mortimer replied. "I'm busy."

"That doesn't matter," Abbie declared. "Gentlemen always have to come when ladies call them."

"I'm busy anyway," said Mortimer.

There was silence for a moment. "What are you doing?" asked Abbie presently, in a lilting tone. Mortimer replied, after reflection, that he was making believe something. When asked what, he admitted that he hadn't decided yet. "I'm probably a pilot on a Boeing 707," he said. "That's probably what I am."

"I'm the pilot's mother," said Abbie, "that goes along with him."

"His mother doesn't go along with him, stupid," said Mortimer. "That just shows how much you know!"

"There's a lady on the plane, isn't there?" Abbie replied. "Well, that's his mother."

"That's the stewardess," said Mortimer in disgust.

"I don't care," said Abbie. "Anyway, she's the one that gives you the things to eat."

"So?" asked Mortimer incautiously.

"So," said Abbie, "you come here and I'll give you things to eat, too."

"What things?" asked Mortimer, approaching warily. But his battle was lost, he was already caught. "Like what?" he asked.

"Like cookies," said Abbie. "Real make-believe cookies.

"And afterwards," she added firmly, "we'll play house."

"Oh, cow!" said Mortimer.

CHAPTER 8

THERE IS nothing sweeter than an afternoon nap;
it is the gentle closing of a door on all the discom-
forts of life, on barking dogs and weariness and
sadness and other people's radios, on loneliness and
children crying. I dreamt of the Hales' big white
high-ceilinged room on Lafayette Street, just below Wanamaker's. Coby was there (he lived up-

stairs) and Ray, both of them quoting Eliza-
bethan poetry to each other, and Guy with his
Rackham, merry as a sprite. It must have been a
party, for there were other friends, and some I
had loved, and one at least who had no business
being there at all—Miranda, or so I thought.

Rowley's lovely lines came through the dream,
in Ray's best voice:

> *"Art thou gone in haste: I'll not forsake*
> *thee.*
> *Runn'st thou ne'er so fast, I'll o'ertake thee.*
> *O'er the dales, o'er the downs, through the*
> *green meadows,*
> *From the fields through the towns to the*
> *dim shadows!"*

"What are you doing here?" I said to Miranda.
"I thought I left you in California."

But she only looked at me. Smiling, she turned,
and put her hand out to Bee, and they walked
away together.

"O western wind," cried Coby, *"when wilt
  thou blow
That the small rain down can rain?
Christ, that my love were in my arms
And I in my bed again!"*

It was the old Coby, glass in hand, with the
wide gestures. But they took no notice of me. I
wanted them to see me, to talk to me, to be glad
I was there. "It was Mingolf," I said, "who stamped
on the tundra."

"No more," said Guy, "no more. Mingolf is dead."
His voice was doleful. "Stay me with flagons," he
said, "and comfort me with apples. . . ."

The dream began to fall apart, like smoke. No,
I thought, no—let me keep it just a little longer.
Miranda . . .

I woke to the sound of a dog howling somewhere in the neighborhood, and with a sadness in
my heart, because Guy was dead, and Bee was
dead, and I wanted to tell Miranda about it. I

went across the hall and knocked on her door, but when she opened it and I saw her standing there, it seemed silly. She always had such a pleasant smile for me; and she was so much alive. "I fell asleep," I said, "and there was something—but I don't remember."

"It's the weather," she said. "If only it would rain; but it won't, not in April any more."

"Miranda," I said suddenly, driven by some need or will not my own, "are you going to marry Claude?"

Startled at first, she turned on me a blank stare which seemed to look through me and beyond me. "Do you think I ought to?" she asked at last.

"I don't know," I said. I felt very tired, and close to my dream, and confused by it. The dog was still howling. I turned to go back to my own apartment, but she took my arm and drew me gently into her room instead. "I need a drink," I said. "Mingolf's dead."

"I need one, too," she said.

She fixed a drink for me, and one for herself, and stirred the ice in her glass with her finger. "Why Claude?" she asked at last, keeping her head bent, and not looking at me. "Why Claude, of all people?"

"Perhaps because he's here," I said. "Perhaps because I don't want to lose you."

She considered for a moment, staring into her glass. "Nobody wants to be lost," she said. "Still, you can be—even when you think you know where you are. Like in a fog on Sunset once; I could have been in Timbuctoo, for all I knew; I could have been anywhere. When I got to Sepulveda, I didn't even know I'd passed it. I could have been anywhere."

She raised her glass. "Here's to Mingolf," she said, "whoever he was. And to Nifty Biddy. He got lost, too."

"With Claude," I said doggedly, "you wouldn't be lost."

She wrinkled her nose at me in a charming

frown. "Maybe I was born in the wrong time of the world," she said. "Or in the wrong season."

I thought she was making fun of me. "Didn't I say that to you once?" I asked. "Yes," she said; "and I never forgot it.

"I keep remembering it," she said. "Because I think it's true."

"It was only talk," I declared. "Only words. You live when you live, that's all."

She shook her head, considering. "Life is such a short time," she said. "A bird's song . . . One ought to be able to live it when one chooses."

"You're not the one who's supposed to talk like that," I said; "I am. And besides—it isn't a bird's song at all."

"A grasshopper's song," she said.

I looked at her, and she looked back at me quietly. "Bee said that once," I said after a while. "Long ago, to somebody . . .

"Was it to Josephine?"

"No," she said. "It wasn't to Josephine."

. . .

A person could be lost was what she had said;
it could happen to anybody, in a fog, or in the
dark. I'd been lost myself one Wednesday night
coming back from Playa del Rey on a road I'd
never taken before. But I was still in California,
and it was still Wednesday; and that was the difference. If Miranda was lost . . .

I finished my drink, and after a while I got up
and went back to my own place. I kept thinking
about the wilderness-stone, and the stream that
never had a name. It could have been the little
green tidal river that poured past Bee's house at
Cohasset. It could have been anywhere.

"Claude," I said to my nephew that night, "if
you are thinking of marrying Miranda . . ."

"Is she dating someone else?" he asked, alarmed.

"Not," I said truthfully, "to my knowledge."
What lay beyond was too disturbing; I preferred
not to think about it. It is one thing to talk about

the power of imagination, and quite another to experience it.

"I've certainly got it on my mind," said Claude. "A fellow doesn't want to be too hasty about a thing like that. You've got to know a person pretty well . . ."

I know this girl. . . .

"Just the same," I said, "I wouldn't wait too long if I were you."

"I won't, uncle," said Claude. "I won't indeed."

A little while later, he said to me: "I'm looking for the right opportunity."

I looked at him in surprise. "To do what?" I asked. "Surely, if you and Miranda are going together . . ."

"I want to be sure," he said.

You don't want to commit yourself yet, I thought; or do you find it too dangerous to say: I love you? It never bothered me when I was your age, and what is more, I always meant it. Still, there were some even then who couldn't give their hearts to anything; they always had to hold back a little.

But they were the exceptions rather than the rule.

Claude wanted to be safe, in an unsafe world. But who is safe, hesitating and not committed?

The opportunity—or what I thought was the opportunity—came a few days later. The four of us—Claude, Miranda, Abbie, and myself—had gone up into Chelly Canyon, back of Sierra Madre. There, on a level ledge above a little stream which is dry nine months of the year, a live oak makes a shady place to sit, and mountain laurel and a few scrub pines give off their small fragrance in the sun. A slice of sky is overhead, blue as silk, and what looks like half the world down below, with the grey haze of the desert far off to the southeast, and to the west the darker haze of the sea.

There have been many hilltops in my life: Sacré-Coeur, Fiesole, a small mountain in the Adirondacks, a hill in Truro among the blueberry bushes.

. . . A hilltop is a good place for lovers: what can a woman say with the world at her feet and heaven overhead? I thought I could charm Abbie at least enough to keep her out of Claude's way.

"Look," I said; "on the mountain over there. That golden bush."

"It isn't really gold," said Abbie.

"Suppose it were," I said. "What would you wish?"

"Why would I wish anything?" asked Abbie.

"Well," I said, "it might come true."

"You mean if it was really gold?"

"Yes."

"Why?"

"Because," I said, "if a thing is true that can't be true, then beggars will ride."

"That's silly," said Abbie.

"I suppose it is," I said; "but there might be some truth in it."

She thought it over for a while. "All right," she said at last; "I'll wish."

She closed her eyes tight and screwed up her little face into a solemn, waiting expression. "I wish," she said; "I wish—that if mother goes away she'll take me with her."

I didn't expect anything like that. "Well, look here," I said uncomfortably, "why should she go away?"

"I don't know," said Abbie simply. "It's just in case she does.

"I have another wish," she said. "Would you like to hear it?"

I said I would. "Well, it's this," said Abbie shyly; "I wish she'd let me cook a shrimp shortcake."

I must have fairly goggled at her. "You can come to my house," I said at last, weakly, "and cook whatever you please."

"Thank you," said Abbie shiningly. And she added with what sounded like a sigh,

"All I can cook so far is hamburgers."

She put her finger to her lips and motioned toward the tree under which Miranda and Claude were talking earnestly. "Mother and Claude are fighting," she said. "They'll probably get married."

They must have raised their voices, because in the sudden wind-hung silence, I heard Miranda say, "Our parents used to believe. They had all kinds of beliefs."

"In what?" he asked.

"In God," said Miranda. "In the country, and the future."

"Do you believe in all that?" asked Claude.

"No," said Miranda unhappily. "But I'd like to."

"They could afford it," said Claude. "There was always an out for them when things went wrong. This time there isn't any."

"What 'out' did my father have," demanded Miranda, "when the Depression came?"

"They had two outs," said Claude bitterly; "those to blame, and those to help them: the bankers to blame, and the Republicans; and the New Deal to help them, and the Democrats. But who's to blame now? You can't find anyone; even

Uncle Edward doesn't know what to think any more. When he was my age, he had it all figured out."

"When he was your age," said Miranda, "the whole world was at spring."

"What do you mean 'at spring,'" said Claude fretfully. "Jumping and frolicking around?"

"I mean that people felt young," said Miranda obstinately. "They knew what it was like to be young."

"Don't you?" asked Claude, I thought a little wistfully.

"I don't know," she said. "I think it went by me, somehow."

"Then what's the good of looking back?" he asked. "What do you think you'll find?"

"Something I've missed, maybe," said Miranda. "Like what?"

"Like joy," she said defiantly.

The word seemed to embarrass him. "Well," he said uncomfortably, "that all depends on what you mean. If you mean the kind of thing they used to write about, with Joy in capital letters, and people always living happily ever after . . . it wasn't like that, and everybody knew it. Mostly, people just got themselves plastered, like Fitzgerald said."

"All right," said Miranda placidly. "I like to dream. Why shouldn't I?"

"I'll tell you why," said Claude. "Because dreaming isn't a way out any more. It's pap and sugar water."

There was a momentary pause. "Take television," he said suddenly. "Do you know why the westerns are so popular? Because there's no happily-ever-after. In a western, a man gets a kiss, and he gets his horse back again, and that's it."

"What does the girl get?" asked Miranda.

"She gets to keep the ranch," said Claude simply.

I thought to myself: they both get security. It hadn't occurred to me before.

Miranda looked out at the great sweep of blue

overhead, and at the broad plain below, melting away into haze. "I wish it was that easy," she said with a sigh. "What if you don't like westerns?"

Claude made a helpless gesture.

"Maybe," said Miranda, "I don't want a ranch. Maybe I want to be loved."

There was silence for a moment. Abbie stared at me with saucer-wide eyes. "Is Mommie controlling him?" she breathed.

"Hush," I said.

Claude cleared his throat. "Well, sure," he said carefully, but a little huskily. "Naturally. Who said you weren't?"

"Nobody said I wasn't," said Miranda. "But nobody said I was."

I didn't hear Claude's answer; he mumbled something, and Miranda sighed and turned away. But Abbie sat with her arms around her thin little knees, staring.

Very soon after that, we went home. There was some polite talk about the view, mostly from Miranda; and Abbie found a dead blue jay on the path and wanted to bring it home with her. Claude alone seemed absent-minded, and once or twice stumbled over a rock or some loose shale. Halfway down the canyon, Abbie drew her mother aside.

"He didn't say he wouldn't marry us, did he?" she asked in an anxious whisper.

Miranda smiled and gave her a pat on the top of her head. "He didn't say he would," she replied.

If I had expected her to be put out about it, I was wrong. If anyone was put out, it was me.

And Abbie, of course.

CHAPTER 9

IT WASN'T hard to understand why Abbie was disappointed; she was afraid of losing Miranda, and thought that once they were married to Claude—both of them, because that was the way she envisaged it—she'd help her mother control him. But why should *I* have felt put out? That was indeed complicated.

Because, if Miranda was in love with Bee, or with the image of Bee, who but I was responsible? And—to be quite honest—hadn't I, through Bee, been making love to Miranda myself? So why set my hopes on her marrying my nephew?

The answer was—I suppose—that she had only to marry Claude to become my niece; and then she and Abbie would be in my life forever, for what was left of it, and I should have a clear proprietary interest, even though a small one, in both of them.

But there was something else.

I was beginning to ask myself a question I couldn't answer. It was this: was it possible that Bee and Miranda were actually closer to each other than I knew, or even guessed; was there something between them that I didn't—and couldn't—understand?

I knew Bee's life, I'd spent so much of it with him, particularly those last years before his death. I knew his friends, and he knew mine. I could ask them, of course—those of them who were still alive, like Ray . . . but ask them what? Ask them if they knew something about Bee that I didn't know?

It seemed impertinent; and what is more, unlikely. I knew Bee's life; I knew all of it.

Or did I? I tried to think back, to remember. . . .

Strange, the things one does remember. I was sitting on the slope of a hill above the old Parsonage in Truro, among the blueberry bushes . . . so it must have been early summer. I was with a great tall, honey-colored girl; I can see her quite clearly in my mind, even now. Her name was Frances; for some reason I called her Toots. The slippery slopes with their tundralike moss quilted with bearberry smelled of thyme and sweet fern; the little hollows of piny woods were below us, and there was fairy grass all around. I remembered the wind and the bright sun, and off to the east the blue Atlantic with a little purple in it, shining in the light. We talked about berries, and sailing, and Fran's college, and how Bee was in Switzerland; my sister had seen him at Chamonix, in the bar of the hotel. "He was with quite a lovely girl," she wrote, "or rather a woman, to whom he didn't introduce us; I believe that she is married, and has a child somewhere, or at least that's the gossip. He told me that they were going out on the glacier in the morning, and he sent you his love. His lady-friend, too, whoever she was—rather sadly, I thought; perhaps you know who it is?"

I didn't know, of course; I would have guessed it to be the woman in Florence, the woman he loved so much and whose name he never told me —except that she had sent me her love, and she didn't know me.

That must have been about the time that the Farnsworths started their art classes in North Truro. There were a lot of painters on the Cape that year, and writers, too; the narrow roads still wound shakily from the Hole right down to Wood End and the last white saw-grass sandy dunes. At night, Land's End light winked across the harbor, and the sunsets flamed off the sea, above Cohasset across the Bay. The Farnsworths had a house on Route 6, with great elms before the door; Dos Passos used to come over from Provincetown, walking all the way along the beaches and up and over the dunes, and stand in the doorway, dark-eager-eyed and sweet and friendly, and always in time for Henka's wonderful cooking. And I remembered how I'd sailed the Henkaberry that year in the Provincetown Wellfleet race, and had come in last. It was a great year for beach-plum jelly.

I have a painting of the town landing on the Pamet, in Truro; it hangs in the bedroom of my apartment above the city. Miranda is quite familiar with it; she speaks of it sometimes as though she had been there herself.

But Bee was climbing mountains . . . and coming—although neither of us knew it—closer to that last one which would be the end of him. Or perhaps not the end; I didn't know then, and I still don't know.

With whom was he? His own letters that summer, from Chamonix, and from Wengen under the shadow of the Jungfrau, told me very little. He was happy, that was clear; the great snow-peaks standing there in the high pure sky excited him. It was from Wengen he sent me the little verse:

> *On the top of a hill*
> *Where the wind blows*
> *Am I—*
> *So still,*
> *So high—*
> *And far below the warm fields doze*
> *All placidly beneath the trees*
> *In green and brown*
> *And shot with bees.*

It was the sort of thing he did; slight, musical, and visual. None of his friends—and certainly none of the critics—thought of Bee as a poet of any importance, even in those days; and among today's reviewers and anthologists his poems are considered—when they are considered at all—little more than nursery rhymes.

Bee wrote from Interlaken: "I have gone up in an aeroplane. It was quite extraordinary, and I wasn't frightened at all. You feel very safe in the air, and steady, except for the bumps, and being seasick.

"Did you know that the Swiss beer is very good? It is lighter than the German. And the croissants and honey at breakfast are better than anywhere in the world. We wake in the morning in the early quiet, and sit in the sun on our balcony and look up at the great gleaming peaks, and feel that clean air on our faces from the snow that always makes me think of cream on hot oatmeal in the morning."

We?

"Did you know that Swiss beer is lighter than German?" I asked Frances, and she said, "No"; and now, more than thirty years later, I asked Miranda if she knew that Swiss beer was very good, and she said that she didn't.

Looking back at it now, I can guess what it was that I was trying to trap her into admitting, and I can see, or at least guess, how much she did admit without my ever knowing it. But how much did she know herself? And what could she have told me, even if she'd wanted to? We move equally in darkness, no matter where—or when.

There was, for instance, the day at Disneyland. It was quite an ordinary day, on the surface—insofar as any day at Disneyland can be considered ordinary. Miranda, the two children, and I went on the ride in the old-fashioned train, complete with everything except the cinders; we took the river journey on the paddle-wheel river boat, and the launch ride down the tropical river. Miranda was gay and happy, laughing at the fearsome crocodiles and the screaming parrots, the drenching waterfalls, and the pilot's monologue, delighted with the color everywhere, the flowers, the sounds, the hum and bustle, the smell of popcorn. Abbie darted here and there, asking questions, peering into shop fronts, buying balloons, staring in horror at the burning log-house and the scalped settler on the bank of the river; while Mortimer, waiting eagerly for the trip around the moon and the flying mono-rail, fortified himself with orangeade and popsicles. It was a bright day, and warm, and the place was full of children.

I was the only one in our little party who could remember from his own past the open-air trolley in which we rode, the ice cream parlors, the apothecary shop, the bandstand in the park. We skipped the Castle of the Sleeping Beauty out of deference to Abbie, who didn't believe in fairy tales, but we rode the monorail, and plunged beneath the sea in the submarine, and throbbed our way into space around the moon and back, without being afraid or getting seasick. "It was swell," said Mortimer; "that blast-off was real good."

However, when it came time to try the Matterhorn, Miranda unaccountably held back. "You go with the children," she said. "I'd rather not."

To be truthful, I, too, would have rather not, but the children were so eager for the ride—the bobsled run—that I hadn't the heart or the courage to say no. I've always hated roller coasters, the dismaying pull upward to the lonely height, and then the chilling drop, the sickening lurch. . . . The young woman at the ticket office assured me that the slopes were gentle; I saw in my mind the meadows of the Engadine. "Are you sure you don't want to try it?" I asked Miranda.

I thought that she looked a little queer. "No," she said quickly, "no . . . really . . ." She kept staring up at the rocky edifice with its snowy peak so like the Matterhorn, almost as though she was frightened of it. When she saw me looking at her, she gave a wavering laugh and turned away. "It's silly," she said, "but I have this feeling. . . ."

"You're not ill?" I asked anxiously. She smiled faintly and shook her head. "No," she said. "You take the children, and I'll meet you here when you come out."

There was a long line in front of the little station which served as the entrance to the mountain run, and it took us quite a while before we were seated in our bobsled made of plastic and rubber, and strapped into our seats, the two children in front and myself behind them. The sled—or the car— stood braked for a last peaceful moment in front of the loading platform while the sleds behind us were filled, and then we were off, down a slight slope and into a tunnel, and then lifted like a bucket up a long steep incline to the top. . . . My heart sank.

I have actually little consecutive memory of the ride itself. At the first rush and drop and sudden bank and swerve I believe (and Abbie told me later) that I let out a single "Oh, God!" and after that I closed my eyes and hung on. I understood that I was caught; I realized suddenly what I was in for, and that there was no escape from it, I was going to have to endure it to the end. Now and then I opened one eye or the other for a brief moment, hoping to catch a glimpse of a gentle valley, or even a quiet glacier, but saw only the stupendous abyss down which we were plunging, or some incredible curve directly ahead, and closed the eye again and gave a small groan. We passed—they tell me—through a number of waterfalls; on one blessed occasion, all too brief, we came out onto a shelf or ledge of the mountain, and I gazed for a second or two with longing at the peaceful scene spread out below me, the blue, pellucid waters of a lake or lagoon, and people going placidly about their business. . . . Then into the tunnel again.

The children were screaming happily at every dip and curve, the way children do, and I paid no attention to it. But suddenly, at one point, as we bent ourselves around a particularly sharp curve and pointed downward at what appeared to be an ice-covered mass of rock, Abbie gave a different cry, a sudden scream of surprise and terror. A moment later I heard her cry, "Mommie!" and saw her bury her face in her hands. I reached forward to put my arms around her; at that moment we came out again onto a quiet shelf on the mountainside. "It's all right," I said; "it's all right, there's nothing to be afraid of. . . . Close your eyes if you want to. . . ."

She pointed back the way we had come and tried to tell me something, but I couldn't hear her. I kept my arms around her; the sled went down another sickening slope, and through a shallow pool, the spray flew up in our faces, and we were back to solid earth again.

But when we stepped out onto the platform, I could see that Abbie was still shaken. Her face was quite pale, and I was afraid that she was going to be sick. I took a deep breath. "It's all over now," I told her. "It wasn't so bad, was it?" "No, sir," said Mortimer; "it was swell. It was real neat. All that snow and everything; it makes you feel hungry, like a hot dog or a soda or something. . . ."

Ordinarily, Abbie would have dealt with him in short order, but now she only gave him a wan, disinterested glance and walked away. She didn't say a word.

Miranda was waiting for us, as she had promised; and as soon as Abbie caught sight of her, she rushed across the pavement, flung herself at her mother's knees and buried her face in her skirts. Miranda looked down at her with a curious expression; I couldn't tell what she was thinking. She didn't say anything, she just tousled Abbie's hair for a moment. If she had intended to ask any questions, she apparently thought better of it.

For the rest of the afternoon, Abbie kept close to her side. She never let her out of her sight; and every now and then she'd reach up to take her by the hand, or touch her skirt. It was almost as though she were afraid of losing her. As though whatever it was she had seen—or thought she had seen—had frightened her.

And the strange thing was that Miranda knew it.

CHAPTER 10

LEONARD IS one of the dear friends of these later years; but he would have fitted in equally well with the old crowd at the Brevoort, all of whom spoke with authority and scholarship and in a ringing style. . . . All, that is, except myself; I was diffident then, and have remained so ever since.

[*129*]

Yet now, since I assume a graver air, my silence passes for reserve.

I found him at his home, practising the fiddle, his brown beard curling over the tailpiece of the instrument. His wife, whom we called Goddess, and his six children were out, taking the air, but the cat was at home, and the dog who snarled at me. "Something is happening to Miranda," I said, "and I don't understand it."

"Well, then," said Leonard, "you've come to the right place, chum, for there's nothing as exhausting in the world as ignorance. Whatever in the world I don't understand, I will guess at, the way I guess at the notes on this cursed fiddle."

"At least," I remarked, "you've had lessons on it; but for what I'm obliged to guess at, there are no teachers."

"Good," said Leonard, putting down the fiddle and drawing up a chair; "let's have it then."

I told him about Bee and about Miranda; I told him everything that had happened so far. When I had finished, he sat in silence for a while, stroking his beard reflectively. "There's the legend of Oisin," he said, "who lived with Niamh for three hundred years, and never had so much as a wrinkle on him the whole time. He wasn't the first to vanish into yesterday—though for the moment I've forgotten the others' names. At the end of it, Oisin came home to Ireland, and had a raging argument with St. Patrick—an old man, and sick for the old ways."

He looked at me from under his brows. "I thought your nephew was the one for Miranda," he said. "What's happened to him?"

"He isn't ready for her," I said. "What he wants is security. If I told him what was happening, he wouldn't believe me."

"You don't know it's happening," said Leonard.

"Of course, I don't," I said. "But I can imagine it. And so can you."

"I could," said Leonard. "I could imagine anything. After all, I once played my fiddle on the streets of London. It was in the Depression, and I had no other way of making a living. It wasn't so much my playing—though I was adequate—as my youth, I being no more than eighteen or nineteen at the time.

"Who could have imagined then that I'd some-day be here by the side of the Pacific Ocean, with six kids and a wife, and no better fiddler than before? How about accompanying me in a bit of the 'Londonderry Air'?"

I sat down at the piano, and he took up his fiddle again and we did a rendition of "Danny Boy" and the Bach Arioso. I cannot say that we were to-gether or in tune with each other. "The thing is," said Leonard, "my beard gets in the way of the little tuning button on the E string, so I let it be and tune the rest to that; and if the piano is off it, why, we're just out of luck."

But it pleased him to play with an accompani-ment. "A man is too much alone in his life," he said, "surrounded as he is by his family that's used to him. He needs a friend now and then to accompany him on the piano. But what's this about your nephew wanting security? It's the curse of the age."

"The way he sees it," I replied, "it's an insecure world, but he clings to it like a barnacle. At least, so he thinks; the fact is, what he's stuck to are the shells of other barnacles. There's a whole generation of them doing the same. But Miranda would rather float away on a current. . . ."

Leonard nodded his head sagely. "I could get lost myself," he said, "between here and the post office, if it wasn't for the road that goes through Hermosa. But tell me—where's a road that goes through yesterday or tomorrow? Maybe there's a spell on the girl, and we should douse her with hyssop, or have her exorcised by the priest. It's when you depart from revealed religion that you're in trouble, chum."

His eyes were bright with mischief. "Revealed to whom?" I asked. "To Moses? Or to Paul?"

"Ah," said Leonard, relishing the argument,

"that's the thing. I'd say to the two of them: from St. Paul to St. Patrick, and so on down to His Eminence, the Cardinal. And the strange thing about it is, it's all based on word of mouth, and a few bits of writing out of people most of us wouldn't sit down to table with. Yet if it hadn't been for men like Elijah and John the Baptist, we'd all be dancing around the Druid Oak to this minute. But they were hard men to get along with."

"They were," I agreed. "One thing Elijah never said, was 'Turn the other cheek.' Or John, either."

"It was the most unminded advice ever given," said Leonard. "It was offered at the time to poor and suffering men, to give them an advantage; and their descendants, once they'd got to the top, laid about them like lunatics and tried to bash everyone in sight. It took a Hindu to teach us the true power of meekness; he turned his cheek so often it broke the heart of the British Empire."

I am always amused at Leonard's explanations. "You talk like the greatest unbeliever in the world,"

I said, "and there's no one with more belief than you!"

"And why not?" Leonard demanded. "I approve of the universe, having a small part in it myself, and I believe in love, and in friendship, and in honor, and in the imagination, and the power of man's soul that is in it. And I believe in the scholars, and in the *shi*, and in a certain island off the coast of Connemara that is said to rise from the sea every once in seven years, and the man that can throw a piece of gold onto it, can step on it himself and so get into eternity through the back door without the nuisance or the agony of death. And I believe that every man has the right to play a bit of the 'Londonderry Air' on the fiddle. Shall we try it again?"

"All right," I said, "but this time let's get in tune with each other before we start."

It went a little better, and after another go at the Bach, and the Lullaby from *Jocelyn*, Leonard put his fiddle down for good, and went to get me a drink. "Look, now," he said when he came back from the kitchen with whisky for me and a huge cup of coffee for himself, "if the girl wants to dream she's in love with a man that's been dead this quarter of a century, I say let her. I had a dream myself when I was a lad, that I'd marry Maeve, the High Queen of Ireland; and so I did, and she turned out to be no other than my wife Hazel. Never interfere with a woman's fancies; she still thinks me an encyclopedia of knowledge, and I wouldn't disabuse her for the world."

We talked for a while of other things, of the books, the novels of the day, which seemed to have turned away from love as a province of the human spirit. "These writers," exclaimed Leonard, "how they hate people, how they hate everything. They cannot get along without alcohol. These angry young men of Britain; do you call that anger? A man like Swift would spit in their eye.

"The thing of it is," he said gloomily, "I'm out of step with world literature; if I could write a book in which a sister nibbles on her brother's knuckle-bones, I'd win a double column in all the reviews, but my wife would throw up on me. And my sons would be eying their sisters askance ever after. But that's the thing that goes today, or else some other kind of devilment from France or Italy. Horror's the word that leads to riches. Do you know who couldn't make a living today?"

"Who?" I asked.

"Mark Twain," said Leonard. "For all the few gruesome bits here and there, in *Huckleberry Finn* and the like."

"He's having a great revival," I said. "How do you explain that?"

"He's dead," said Leonard, "and we respect our monuments—particularly when they've been honored by foreigners. Besides, Twain was a little wicked in an innocent age, and that gives us an affection for him."

We talked about the past. "I wonder," he said, "did anyone ever go through fancier doings than ourselves? Two great wars (though I was a bit young for the first)—to say nothing of the business in Korea; two revolutions, and a Depression. It's enough to give a man indigestion. And yet, when I think of the bad times we've had, I can feel a lightness of spirit, compared with what I feel about the present. I was a street-corner musician in the Depression, but nobody hated me for it; the worse I played, the more people wanted to share with me the little they had. There's nothing like a disaster to bring out the best in people, for a while, anyway."

He took a sip of his coffee and wiped his moustache with the back of his hand. "Though I wouldn't like to see it go on for too long," he said. "The human spirit is a delicate plant; it can split a stone in two, but it can die in a hurry once the worms get at it.

"And worms," he concluded, "are what are at it, chum—make no mistake. The young people who come to see me sometimes—the dullness of them!

Without curiosity, without a thought in their heads for what's beyond their noses, their faces like a closed book, and all of them alike as peas in a pod waiting for something to shock them out of their apathy. They have no merriment at all.

"Naturally, I'm not speaking of my own, who are altogether different, and too young to be counted anyway."

It is true, I thought: we have anger, or what passes for it, though as Leonard said, it would be scarcely recognizable to men of another age; and a kind of mirth, loud, ungentle, and unkind. But we have no gaiety; and for that reason we have no gallantry. What laughter there is, is harsh and frightening or else sly and self-conscious.

Yet did we ever have so many people telling us how to live? Writing their How-to books for adults —how to be healthy, or wealthy, or wise . . . how to make money in real estate, how to be married, how to make friends, how to find God. Have we ever had so many critics telling us how to write novels and how to write plays—and many of them not even promoted from the sports section, the way they used to be, but full professors themselves at the colleges and schools?

Who reads today for the joy or the love of it? Not the young, certainly; indeed, many of them have trouble reading at all. When I was a child I was taught my ABC's in the old way, and once I'd learned them I had them forever, with a few trifles of misspelling here and there. By the time I was ten, I was reading Henty, and Scott, and Smollet, too, which I wasn't supposed to read at all, and was kept under a kind of lock and key in the bookcase. But by the time I'd grown up, it had been decided that the ABC's weren't good for children, it was better for them to look at a picture and at the puzzling scrawl of letters under it, and make a flying guess. In this way, a generation grew up able to read the paintings in the caves of the Dordogne, or the pictographs in *Life* or *Look*, but not the works of Joseph Conrad. The sad fact is they are not aware of their loss since the stories of Conrad are being translated into television along with Sophocles and the works of Erle Stanley Gardner.

Nobody laughs. . . . I am reminded of Calaf's great aria in the last act of *Turandot:* "Nessun dorma." No one sleeps, O Princess, for no one knows my name. They must discover it by dawn, or pay the penalty which is death. It is not so different today: if we do not find the right name for Love, we, too, will have to face the consequences.

Late in the afternoon the Goddess returned with all her children, and little Arabella flung herself across the floor into my lap, and exploded into love like a flower. She is only three; the professors haven't caught her yet.

CHAPTER 11

ONE CAN throw hyssop on a witch—with what re-
sults there may be—but how does one exorcise the
past? It wasn't all love and goodness, even though
I look back at it with love; there was bitterness,
too, and death, and mistakes in the body politic.
The easy times came to an end in the fall of '29.

[*142*]

We were not given any guarantee of survival, but we survived, God's smaller creatures in particular.

For instance—Mr. Rosenberg. He came trudging up the stairs of my apartment house one day back in '31—a small, discouraged, hungry man, shabby but obstinately neat, and carrying a violin case. The Depression was already more than a year old: men were selling apples on the streets, and looking in vain to a government that had nothing to offer them, not even courage. It was the worst time: no one saw anything ahead but fear and evil, the collapse of the world as we had known it, and the influence of Prohibition.

Who can see what lies ahead, for himself or his country? Within a year Roosevelt would be in the White House, the banks would be closed, nobody would have anything at all, and for a while at least everybody would feel relieved. For the first time, people would be obliged to trust one another.

I don't remember why Mr. Rosenberg came to see me, or what he thought I could do for him. He handed me his card, on which was printed rather than engraved, the words:

MORRIS ROSENBERG

CONCERT VIOLINIST

FIRST PRIZE, PARIS CONSERVATORY, PARIS, FRANCE

SOLOIST WITH PITTSBURGH SYMPHONY,

PITTSBURGH, PA.

"MORRIS ROSENBERG WAS THE SOLOIST

OF THE EVENING."

—GALESBURG DEMOCRAT

I remember that I asked him to come in, and offered him a cup of tea and some little cakes that I had been saving all week for the most beautiful woman in the world. I remember that I left the room for a moment, and that when I returned, the plate was swept clean and the cakes were all gone; they were in Mr. Rosenberg's pocket. Poor soul, there was nothing else I could do for him, and after a while he left. I heard, later on, that he took to playing his violin on street corners, while people dropped coins into his hat. Where and how he lived, I don't know—although now that I come to think of it, I believe that he slept in some shed or shelter in the Park during the spring and through the summer.

I have been trying to remember the panic and the bitterness of those years, but—like Leonard—I remember something else: a lightness, almost a gaiety of spirit, reckless if you like, and even desperate at times, but brotherly. We blamed the rich, and at the same time we felt sorry for them, because they were not rich any more. To be a poet was to be no worse off than a stockbroker; for the first time, Bee's aunt and uncle regarded him with respect because his world—unlike theirs—was in no smaller pieces than before.

Those were bad days for bankers and Republicans, but good days for the arts. The painters were busy up and down across the land, painting murals in post offices; the pay was small, but how many of them were accustomed to wealth? Every city had its Little Theater at government expense; there were no fortunes to be made, but actors were allowed to act, and kept from starving, and for many of them that was as near heaven as they were ever likely to get. Book sales flourished, even fiction (except during the bank holiday), and the motion-picture palaces were full. Both Stephen Vincent Benét and Edna St. Vincent Millay had been elected to the National Institute of Arts and Letters a year or so earlier; and at the Opera, Jeritza sang Tosca lying on her stomach. There was a lot to be thankful for.

At the Algonquin, where I sometimes lunched with Henry James Forman, or Ben Lucien Burman, the Round Table met as usual: Aleck Woollcott, dean of drama critics, plump and mischievous as a wasp; Heywood Broun, like a large, untidy bear; Robert Benchley in his sad, sweet, endless alcoholic search for the world's kindness, with his two friends, Dorothy Parker (in the vain search of pity for herself) and Peggy Leech, cool, tall, fair, some-day-to-be historian and Pulitzer Prize winner. And

Deems Taylor, friendly and wary, and Edna Ferber and George Kaufman, the warm, indignant heart, and the clever bones. And the immensely tall Robert Sherwood, waiting patiently for his glory.

Konrad Bercovici was there at a table along the wall, the dark, fierce, gentle gypsy; and Edith Haggard, small, golden, Victorian, a rose petal made of steel and known to her friends and clients as Butch. Hendrik van Loon drew his pictures on the tablecloth; Frank Case, whose tablecloth it was, admired them.

All these I remember, some of them my friends: I salute them across the years, across the silence. One does not grow old without friends—or without enemies. My enemies are mostly among the middle-aged, the neither-old-nor-young . . . those who have lost their heart's marrow, and have not found anything else to take its place. Poor weary souls, I wish them a joy they do not have.

Bee and I walked through the city that year. We saw the long lines in front of the soup kitchens, we watched the apple-sellers, we knocked on the doors of speakeasies and whispered the necessary words. At the House Of Lords, Prince Michael Romanoff shook Bee's hand and borrowed ten dollars from him, an insignificant sum. To me, the make-believe prince was a figure of wonder—a man who lived his own dream so thoroughly, and with such engaging joy, that other people came to believe—or almost believe—it. Now Mr. Romanoff is in the restaurant business, and the dream has grown a little thin, but to me it still has a certain poetry.

Later I came to know and love the real prince and princess, who live on Cape Cod. We used to gather in front of a great fire on the beach and sing the old songs and chanteys, while the stars sailed overhead, and the young girls dreamed with the firelight on their faces.

"Love, oh love, oh careless love . . ."

In the Park there were signs and portents; where the old Reservoir used to be, at Eighty-fourth

Street, there was a shallow depression now, on the dirt floor of which scores of shacks had been erected in defiance of regulations; built of bits of wood, flattened tin cans, old, battered doors, pieces of canvas, and even cardboard, they formed a little city of their own, a community of the homeless and the hopeless. One day we came on a tool shed, used for storing some of the machinery of the Park Department, and looking inside, saw an eighteenth-century bed, elaborately carved, and a small stove. A frightened girl peered out at us; we smiled and waved and passed on.

But later Bee went back with a chicken sand-wich and some cocoa. He told me that three people were living in that shed; from his description, it is possible that one of them was Mr. Rosenberg.

Spring came to New York, the grass in the Park took on its look of dandelions, the cherry trees foamed pink and white along the east wall, and the children sailed their boats in the pond at Seventy-second Street. The air was clear and the sunlight yellow on buildings which rose into the sky with an air of triumph and repose.

"I am going back to Europe again," said Bee, "before too long. I may never see you again, Edward."

"Why not?" I demanded. "Do you expect to stay there forever?"

"I might," said Bee. "I have a feeling about it.

"Besides, living is cheaper. . . ."

A little later he said to me: "Do you think there might be only one woman for a man to love in all the world?"

"Do you mean for all his life?" I asked. And when he nodded his head, "I don't know," I said. "I haven't lived all my life yet.

"Ask me thirty years from now."

Bee sighed. "Have you ever looked across a room," he asked, "and seen somebody whom you would have loved if only you'd met her a little sooner, as at another party?" "Or perhaps later," I said. "Yes," he said, "at another time, or in another place.

"And you wonder who she is, and what she is, and where from, and toward what tomorrow . . ."

"Married, perhaps," I said, "to someone else, and you too late . . ."

"Or too early," he said. "And then what, Edward?"

"Why then," I said, shrugging my shoulders, "you must depend on charms and spells."

"Shall I seek out witches?" asked Bee. "Search for the hungry sorcerers, and grasp the philosopher's stone?"

"The wilderness-stone," I said. "Steve's wilderness-stone."

"It's all the same," said Bee. "To build 'an outcast house of apple-twigs Beside a stream that never had a name.'"

"It depends," I told him, "on whether you believe that love is immortal."

"Or whether," he added gravely, "you think that God is love."

We had been playing till then—or so I thought; but I was suddenly tired of playing. "Well," I said flatly, "I don't. God is as much love as a spider. In a man, He is man, and in a star, He is fire. In a spider, He is a spider; and in space, He is space."

Bee looked at me curiously, and—I thought—a little sadly. I think now that he must have wanted to avoid this discussion. "In a man, He is man," he repeated slowly. "But surely—man is a manifestation of God, Edward; and surely, to show yourself in any form is to show your love for that form. And so—in His manifestations, God must show His love, whether in man or woman, or in fire and space."

"And in the spider?"

"And in the spider."

"Who can love a spider?"

"Only God."

"Then God's love is different from man's," I declared; to which Bee replied unhappily,

"I never said it wasn't."

He laid his hand on my arm. "I wish I could tell you," he began; "I wish I could tell you. . . ."

He sighed again, and lapsed into silence. "Tell me what?" I asked, but he didn't answer.

After a while I began to talk about the past, about the doings and the whereabouts of our friends. There had been some changes, some of those who had been living abroad had come home again now that money was scarce, and there were some new writers to be reckoned with; among other things, it was the year of Mr. Huxley's *Brave New World*. Many of the new young men and women adopted an irritable manner, or a prophetic tone, and inquired into the benefits of socialism; under the circumstances, this was scarcely to be wondered at. The southern school was still centered at Chapel Hill; Mr. Faulkner had not yet arrived at greatness.

The generation was growing older. Coby was the editor of a magazine, and Ray was thinking of going west with his actress wife. "Nothing lasts forever," I said.

Bee made a puzzled gesture with his hands.

"Then where does it go?" he asked. "It can't just disappear—vanish—as though it had never been. It must be somewhere. . . . All of it—space and fire, the trilobite, Adam and Eve, and my own love. . . ."

"Was it she," I inquired, "who was with you in Chamonix?"

Bee stared at me in surprise. "How did you know that?" he asked.

I told him that my sister had written to me. "She said the lady was attractive," I declared, "and married."

"Yes," Bee said. "She is both."

"My sister also said that you didn't introduce her."

He looked off into the distance; he seemed uncertain, and a little wary. "It was all rather confusing," he said. "It always is when we're together."

"You might at least have introduced her," I said.

"I couldn't," he replied. "There was no way."

"And shall I never get to meet her, either?"

He shrugged his shoulders. "Perhaps," he said. "I don't know. . . . Some day . . ."

"At least," I said, "tell me this much: how did you get to meet her yourself? And where, and when?"

"When?" said Bee in a puzzled way; "I'm not sure. Or where. It was just that one day she was there. Do you remember the morning we sat on the sidewalk and watched the moon go down and the sun come up over the city? It was about then, I think . . . or a little later. . . ."

We were on the Mall. The long, shadowed walk with its trees and benches, where a few children were still skating up and down before their suppertime, was already fading into dusk, filled with slanting, dusty light like a cathedral. Pigeons cooed and strutted at our feet, searching for crumbs or peanuts, or for one another; from the children still playing their solitary games came shrill, occasional cries. To the south the city rose like a range of mountains, lofty and mysterious in the declining sky.

For a moment I thought of all the great cities of the world, standing in their history: Babylon with its sky-hung terraces, Nineveh of the Lion Gates, Palmyra rising from the golden sands, Persepolis, Thebes, Troy of the topless towers, Corinth with its face to the wine-dark sea, Carthage strewn with salt . . . all, all gone by, into the night behind us. . . .

I must have been dreaming, for when I turned to speak to Bee, he wasn't there. I saw him at a little distance, walking back in the direction from which we had come. He was not alone; someone was with him, her arm in his—a slender figure in a summer dress, without a hat. It was strange for that time of year in New York. Neither she nor Bee looked back at me; I didn't see her face. In the twilight, it seemed to me that her hair was elm-colored.

CHAPTER 12

I say that I must have been dreaming, but I was awake at the time. In my actual dreams I often dream of the past, but the events are confused; once I found myself dancing at the old Casino in the Park. The music was the same, Eddie Duchin's band was playing "Time On My Hands," but I was dancing with Miranda instead of Edna.

At other times I am pursued by lions, or else enormous waves approach me from the sea, higher than hills. They have no effect on my health; I sleep well, and wake up refreshed, or at least no worse off than before; and my analyst friends tell me that I am not remembering the Flood, or my life in the Cro-Magnon period.

But Miranda's dreams at this time were different; they seemed to tire her, sometimes when I saw her on the street or at the market I noticed that her face was drawn. And I thought that at such times she looked at me with a curious expression, almost as though she wasn't sure who I was, or had expected me to be someone else.

Then one day she said to me: "Edward, what was the name of the hotel in Chamonix?"

I stared at her in surprise. "I have no idea," I said. "Why do you ask?"

She didn't answer directly, but countered instead with another question.

"Wasn't your sister there?"

"Why yes," I said. "Did I tell you?"

"I suppose you did," she said. "I guess you must have."

"Still," I said, "why Chamonix?"

She made a vague gesture. "I don't know," she said; and then, suddenly,

"I think I was there."

"In a dream?"

"I suppose so," she said. "How else?"

How else indeed? There didn't seem to be any other explanation. If I had told her about my sister having written to me from Chamonix, she had perhaps some reason to remember it. . . . But had I? After all, that was long ago; why should I have mentioned it to Miranda thirty years later? I wondered if I had.

As I look back on it now, it seems to me that I was a little slow in understanding; that I, who believe—and did believe—so strongly in the power of imagination to turn time backwards or forwards —reacted in a curiously matter-of-fact way to what

I didn't comprehend. Or did I in fact believe as strongly then as I do now? Perhaps not; I have had more cause since.

I think the first time I felt the true chill go through me was when Miranda told me how she'd found herself in an old, walled garden, in a place she had never seen before. "There was a terrace," she said, "and statues; and it was night, but the birds were singing very beautifully. Like our own mockers. But it wasn't California; it wasn't anywhere I knew."

That was when something inside me gave a shiver; I felt cold and daring and a little ridiculous. "You weren't alone," I said.

"No," she admitted; "there were people, and one of them was called Edward, I think."

I took a deep breath. "You didn't know who Edward was?" I asked.

"No," she said calmly. "Should I have?"

"You might have heard of him," I said.

"I think I did," she said; "somewhere, later. But I didn't know him."

"You never met him," I said.

She looked at me strangely. "How did you know?" she asked.

"I was that Edward, Miranda," I said.

For a long while she stared at me without speaking. "What a strange dream," she said at last. "It was so real."

"Yes," I said, "real enough."

"I was with Bee," she said.

"I know."

After that, there was a difference in Miranda's attitude toward me. We had always been friendly to each other, from our first meeting, but now we were drawn together in a new way; she seemed to turn to me for comfort, as though the mere fact of my presence helped to allay whatever terrors stalked her. In the deepening mystery into which she felt herself sinking, I was at least tangible proof of something real: I had known Bee, I had known those places, those things had happened. Bee was gone, but I was still there; I was a witness.

I noticed, too, how when she looked at Abbie,

her face took on a wondering and sorrowing expression, loving and a little helpless; I have seen that same expression on the faces of travelers as they stood at the rail of a ship bound on a long voyage, waving good-bye, and already a little homesick for what they have left behind.

Claude was distracted those days, what with the foreign news and the ever new developments in real estate which he considered little short of miraculous. He and Miranda were still dating, but more and more often she preferred to stay home by herself, and I could see that Claude was beginning to lose his assurance. Now when he attempted to discuss the day's events with her, he found her, as he put it, "not with it."

I told him—perhaps a little irritably—that it was his own fault. "You had your chance," I said, "in Chelly Canyon. What happened? Nothing seemed to come of it."

"I don't know," he said glumly. "I thought she was fond of me. I guess I didn't measure up."

"To be fond is scarcely enough," I said. "A woman wants to love and to be loved."

He threw his hands up in the air. "I told her," he said; "I mean—I said it to her. I told her I cared."

"You said it the way you felt it," I told him, "in a sort of mumble. She's waiting for someone to say it to her in fire and glory. . . . With love and wonder."

He stared at me for a moment in open amazement. My nephew has never been able to reconcile himself to the fact that—when younger—I was considered a poet by my contemporaries; and I could see that he was embarrassed for me. "Was that the way you used to say it, Uncle Edward?" he asked with what struck me as a sickly smile.

"It is indeed," I said firmly.

He shook his head in a pitying way, and for a moment I felt as though I was the young man, and he the old one. "Things have changed," he said. "Things like love and forever; things like that. It all went out with the movies. It went out after Hiroshima."

"Why Hiroshima?" I asked. "What had that particular death to do with it?"

"It sort of makes you think," said Claude simply. "It makes you think: what was the good of all that love and wonder?"

I have to confess that sometimes I ask myself the same question.

And yet—that, too, that wonder—was part of the world's history. And we must try to see that history whole, like a great painting not yet finished, or a mural still unfolding itself upon the wall. Wherever joy and love and hope are to be found, there, however small the stroke on the enormous canvas, there is a color. The dream of Siddhartha is there, and the teachings of Jesus; they brighten a history in which there has been much sadness and disappointment. Compared to the

Sermon on the Mount, the poems of my generation
were small potatoes; but they were written—many
of them—with love, and people will go back to
them.

If they live. One cannot altogether avoid a sus-
picion that they may not. Such hate as has been
voiced lately by the Chinese and the Russians has
been heard in the past, more than once, and from
other voices; it never led to anything very good.

And if you go to the man in the street, he will
tell you that hate is real, and that love is not. I have
an uncomfortable feeling that Claude would agree
with him. At the same time, I am sure that Claude
doesn't hate anything; and perhaps this is what is
wrong with him. He doesn't hate war, or poverty,
or death; he only fears them.

Perhaps the ability to hate is what makes a man
—or a nation—great. *Carthago delenda est.* What
a melancholy thought.

Could it not be the ability to love? To wonder,
and to love . . . ?

If Claude had any dreams at this time, he didn't talk about them. I presume that he had; the doctors tell us that it's not the sleep but the dream which rests us—by allowing us to exercise our hostilities as well as our fantasies.

However, Abbie had had a dream; she dreamt that she was building a house with her mother. "It was in a pretty place," she told me, skipping along beside me on the way to the corner market to buy Miranda a loaf of bread and some cans of soup. "It was all green, and flat, and there was a lot of long grass that was prickly and speary, and there was a beach, a big wide beach with white sand, and the sea. Only, the sea was different, it was greener in near the shore, and it was clear and clean; and further out it got very blue, and the sun shone on it. And there was a big brown house near the shore, and there was an orchard behind it, and a kind of river ran past it. It came from the sea, and it was green, too, and clear, and it made a rivery noise."

"Which house were you building?" I asked. "The big brown one?"

"No," said Abbie; "that was built already and people lived in it. Mommie was building another one in the orchard, and I was helping her. There was a little boy there with a funny name: I think he was a friend of mine."

She took my hand and we walked along in step together for a while. "Do you remember the bug," she said shyly, "the one with the seven squirly legs?"

"I thought you didn't believe in him," I said.

"I know," she agreed. "But maybe I do now."

"Why?" I asked. "What made you change your mind?"

"I don't know," she said. "I guess I just dreamed it."

I no longer had any doubt that in some way or other Miranda had seen Bee and had talked to him —more than once. And now—Abbie, too? The house she had described, with the orchard behind it . . . that had been Bee's house. And the beach, and the river—could that have been anywhere but Cohasset?

We bought what we'd set out to buy and started home again. The white apartment houses, the dusty palms, stood firm and solid in the hot California light. There was no cool New England sky, no apple-green stream. . . .

"I hear that you and Abbie have been building a house," I said to Miranda on our return. I tried to make it sound inconsequential. "Well," I said, "that's better than chicken coops."

She gave me a troubled glance. "Did she tell you her dream?" she asked; and when I said yes, she added in flat, level tones,

"We were there together, Edward."

"Yes," I said; "I know. In her dream; she told me so."

Miranda hesitated; she kept her face turned from me, but I thought that she was more disturbed than she wanted me to know. "It was my dream," she said at last. "We were together in mine."

I was not surprised. "Do you know where you were?" I asked.

"No," she said in a low voice; "I don't know. Our house was in an apple orchard. There were twigs and branches on the ground, and we were building it together."

"And the river?" I insisted. "Did it have a name?"

"It had no name," said Miranda. "It never had a name."

CHAPTER 13

THERE WAS no question any more; I knew now
Miranda was the mysterious woman in Bee's life.
That this made it all the more mysterious was in
no way relevant: as Leonard pointed out to me,
one must be willing to go all the way in one's beliefs, or not believe at all. "Never ask for the facts,

chum," he said; "when you get them you may not know what to do with them. Don't expect the Lord to keep time with a mortal chronometer; He has as much right to get the snows of yesterday mixed up with next winter's blizzards as any other poet.

"And if it seems a bit unearthly to you, the whole of Christianity is pretty unearthly, too, when you come to think of it—looked at, that is, in the light of reason and experience. But they're poor guides to reality, as you've said yourself, or to the grand design. We've had all kinds of strange doings in Ireland these two thousand years; and if Cuchulainn himself came in the doorway this minute and asked for a bit of oat cake, I'd only be sorry I didn't have it to give him, and myself with this elegant lobster salad instead."

"At least," I said, "you'd be surprised."

"I've been surprised since birth," said Leonard. "It never fazed me."

The occasion was a dinner party at my apartment for six of us—the Wibberleys, Claude, Miranda, and a young man by the name of Alexander Badmeiler. Mr. Badmeiler was a writer: he had written a novel which had already been bought by the movies. He was unable to tell us very much about it, due to the presence of ladies.

"Of course," he said modestly, "I don't expect them to film the book as written. That is, I don't expect them to do justice to the strength of my work." He made a deprecating gesture. "For a while," he said, "I thought I wouldn't let them have it at all . . . why sell my soul for money? You know how it is. Actually, what do I need? Just freedom, and some good music. But then I thought, what the hell, why fight success?"

He turned to Leonard. "You sold one to the movies, too, didn't you?" he asked. "How much did you get for it?"

Leonard bent his full fierce blue-eyed brown-bearded face on him, not unlike Zeus glaring down from Olympus. "I was given the Victoria Cross," he said, "and the Lake Isle of Innisfree."

But Mr. Badmeiler wasn't listening. "I got fifty thousand dollars," he said, and reached for another helping.

I had read Mr. Badmeiler's book. In it, the characters never left one bar expect to move on to the next, never got out of bed except to fall into another. They drank and vomited and whored their way through seven hundred pages, and the only word that Mr. Badmeiler never used was the single word: love.

He wondered if we had seen his press notices; he had had, he told us, a tremendous press. "A great talent," said the *Saturday Review*. It was generally considered a depressing piece of work by those who had actually read it.

It was different in Hollywood, where very few people read at all. "They're going to put a lot of high-priced stars into it," he said. "They think it'll get an Academy Award."

"Boy!" murmured Claude.

I knew what he was thinking: of all the things

that fifty thousand dollars would buy. Security, or escape—either one: a big house-trailer in which a man could live anywhere in the country, far away from the bombed-out cities, or two lots in the Landover Development which could easily double in value in ten years.

I thought of that army of the desperate and the poor who have no help from the great powers of the world—no lobby before Congress, no friends in the seats of the mighty—who, alone, with only a pencil, a brush, a mallet, with only their minds and their hearts, face the world of bankers and traders, of merchants and Rotary Clubs, of taxes and pensions, social security, group insurance, and Federal housing. Poor Don Quixotes . . . or Roland winding his lonely horn in Roncesvalles.

Or a Badmeiler.

He was winding his horn above the salad and the dessert. "I had three studios bidding for it," he said.

But there was something uncertain and even

touching about him; it was obvious that he had never expected to be great. And I could see that his literary style was natural to him, that he lived the way he wrote. After dinner he sat on the floor and peered soulfully at Miranda over a large glass of whisky, ice, and water. "Hey there," he remarked from time to time; "hey."

Miranda regarded him absently. She was obviously indifferent to him, but he worried Claude who resented his success and the bold and careless way he looked at her. "Hey," he said, waving his glass; "they're giving a party for me at the Beverly Hilton."

I felt suddenly sorry for Mr. Badmeiler. Probably no one had ever given a party for him before; it must have seemed like Christmas and the Fourth of July to him, all of a sudden life was pinwheels and sparklers and spun-glass angels. His second book, I thought, was going to disappoint everybody, himself most of all.

"Yes, ma'am," said Mr. Badmeiler; "I'm having

lunch tomorow at Romanoff's with my producer."

"What you ought to do," said Claude, "is buy a house out here. Then you'd have something."

Mr. Badmeiler gave him an owlish look and sighed suddenly. "I miss Brooklyn," he said. "This damned endless sunlight."

Yes, I thought; I, too, miss the autumn skies, bright with dying summer, or heavy with coming snow.

"I miss the boys in the back room," said Mr. Badmeiler. He held his glass out to be filled, and I filled it for him. "What I mean is," he said, "all these people with sunburned faces.

"Not," he added, "that the women are bad-looking." And holding up his glass in Miranda's direction, he intoned,

"Hey there."

Hazel Wibberley from across the room gave him a motherly glance. "Hey yourself," she said.

"I like it here," he announced. "My next book's going to be about a bullfighter. Like Hemingway."

"Ah," said Leonard, "Hemingway. Now there's a great sentimentalist for you. The only one of any consequence in the country."

Mr. Badmeiler goggled up at him. "A sentimentalist?" he croaked. "Hemingway? Papa? You out of your mind?"

"The dictionary," said Leonard, "defines sentiment as an appeal to the emotions in literature and art. That takes in about everything from *Hamlet* to 'The Star-Spangled Banner'; but let's narrow it down a bit to what we usually mean when we speak of sentiment or sentimentality. Well, now— this man Hemingway is a fine writer, which I don't for a moment deny, and has been brimming over with the fear of death and with pity for himself ever since the beginning. It's given him a kind of desperate courage; but death and pity ride his books like bulls. Just tell me this: when did he ever get the girl, or the fish? Do you know that one, *Across the River and Into the Trees?* It's not considered his best; but I believe he was never more open in his life. There's the boy of his own heart, this Colonel Cantwell, and some very good facts about duck shooting. The writer I have no use for is the one who gets the girl and doesn't know what to do with her."

"And who would that be?" asked Mr. Badmeiler a little thickly. "Anyone knows what to do with a girl."

He got slowly to his feet and looked around for Miranda. "Where is she?" he asked plaintively. "Hey there."

But Miranda was no longer in the room. I thought I caught a glimpse of her on the balcony. "Excuse me," I said, rising.

"You leaving?" he asked.

"No," I said; "just a breath of air."

He drew a long sigh. "Somewhere," he said, "I think I lost the way."

Perhaps I misunderstood him. "Straight ahead," I told him, "and the second door to the left."

He looked after me with a plaintive expression. "Anyone knows," he said. "Don't thev?"

I slipped out on the balcony . . . but I hadn't expected the view to be so different. There should have been the jewel-lights of the boulevards below us, the glowing traffic signals, the blazing neon signs—and not the scattered few lights of a village and the snowy moonlight of a mountain rising at the end of a valley, silent and ghostly in the night.

And Bee shouldn't have been there . . . How young he looked! "I thought you'd come," he said, "sooner or later."

I recognized his voice, with the little cracked laugh in it. It had been so long since I'd heard it. "Where are we?" I asked; and my own voice sounded muffled and strange.

"In Lauterbrunnen," he said; "looking up the valley to Wengen and the Jungfrau. Don't you remember?"

Yes, I thought, I remember: it was the last time we were ever abroad together, the time I left him there and went on by myself to Frankfurt where there was a young woman whose eyes were even bluer than Bee's, and who smelled deliciously of tea. The tea turned out to be a perfume, delicate and sweet; its name was Tweed. Strange, what one remembers. She must be a grandmother by now, I thought.

And I remembered, too, that Bee had been expecting someone. I remembered how restless he had seemed, with a kind of desperate eagerness. . . . I gazed out at the quiet, unreal valley, with its cold still air, and the great mountain pale and snowy in the night. "We got as far as the Eiger Glacier," I said, remembering; "from Little Scheidegg." "In a funicular," said Bee.

He looked so young, so moonlight young, with the night flowing around him; and I felt a great sadness. Were we really like that? I wondered; I, too? So starlight eager, so fragile, so quick to perish. . . .

"I've asked her to come to live with me," said Bee. "But it's very difficult."

Difficult indeed, I thought; that must be the most difficult of all voyages. "You come, too, Edward," he said. "Then we'll all be together."

It was so much the Bee I had known, wilful as the wind. I heard the old infectious gaiety in his voice. "Don't be absurd," I told him gently. "I'm an old man. You wouldn't want me."

And then, even as I spoke, it all moved away from me, and I was old and lonely and bewildered and in another time, looking at something I had no business to see—Bee and Miranda together and unaware of me, leaning on a balcony in Lauterbrunnen, under the snow of the Jungfrau. . . .

I was watching Miranda's face, the helpless, shining look on it, and Bee bending over her, pleading—

"Come with me!"

And her whisper: "Oh, my dear. . . . How can I?"

He threw up his bright head in a way I remembered. "Why is it like this?" he cried. "We should have been together all these years. These few years . . ."

And Miranda's whisper: "Out of all the world, only you."

[*181*]

"Out of all the world," he said.

"How can I love you?" cried Miranda. "And yet, I do! No one has ever been so far away."

"Even the stars are nearer," he said.

"Even the stars."

"There has been only this one wonder," he said, "from the beginning."

"I know," she said. "From the morning when the moon went down over the park."

"I whistled you to me. I called you home like a peregrine."

She smiled gently into the darkness. "I followed you home," she said. "You didn't have to call me."

"But I did," he insisted. "I saw your face behind my closed eyes, and I willed you into the world with me."

"I, too. Perhaps it was both of us."

"Then it was both of us. From the beginning."

"In the beginning," said Miranda, "all I wanted was to be happy, for a moment, for a little while. But then I fell in love. At first it was only with a memory—something I heard, something I was told; not even mine. And after a while, it was mine.

"I love our times together," she said. "Even though they have to end."

"Don't let them end. Stay with me."

"I want to. Oh, I want to!"

A breath of air, cold as snow, enveloped us for a moment, drifting down from the mountain. She raised her hands in a sudden little gesture, touching and helpless. "Forever," she said.

"Stay," he begged. "Stay with me. . . ."

"I can't," she whispered. "This is all. I cannot stay."

"All?" he cried. "This drop of time? This splinter of eternity? Did we just happen—in the wrong season of the world?"

Bee's figure was fainter now, and I could see traces of tears on Miranda's cheeks. The valley of the Jungfrau was hazy; the lights of Wengen seemed to waver in the mist. Was that the mountain there, hovering in the sky, or the new apartment building on Wilshire?

"I didn't choose it," she cried. "I didn't choose this time to be alive! This now, this here. . . ."

"Then come to me," he pleaded. "Be with me where I am."

"Oh, yes," she breathed; "yes!"

I put my hand on hers, that was cold as ice. "Here is where you are," I told her. "This is your now, and here."

"No," she exclaimed; "no! I don't want it to be!" But she neither felt me nor saw me. "Oh," she cried, holding out her arms to him, "how can I come to you? How can I be with you?"

I could scarcely see him any longer, he was no more than a shadow in the wind against the nightglow of the boulevards. "There is no single season," he said.

Behind us someone stepped noisily across the sill and onto the balcony. Far off across the city the red riding-lights of a plane winked slowly downward in the sky like a dying firecracker. "Aren't you cold," asked Claude, "out here in the dark?"

And Bee's voice like a thin whisper, hardly more than a remembered sound:

"There is more than that to eternity."

"Yes," said Miranda bravely. "There is."

"What?" asked Claude. "What is there?"

She turned and looked at him, seeing him, and seeing me, too, as if for the first time: a blank, dazed look, like someone out of sleep, or from a long journey. She gave a little gasp like a sob, and shivered suddenly, and swayed, and I put out my hand to steady her. "It's cold," she said. "I'm going in."

We went back, blinking in the sudden light. The warmth, the remembered reality of the room enfolded me, shaken as I was; the world outside was a dream, nothing had happened, nothing had ever happened. Here were the solid things I owned, that I had bought and loved and used in those thirty years since Lauterbrunnen, each with its history, its memories and claims: my tables, my chairs, my lamps, pictures, books. . . . Here were my witnesses, not of eternity, but of a single season in the world.

"Our friend," said Leonard, "has been telling us of the resounding success of his book in the countries of Europe. They are particularly partial to it in England, he says, where they enjoy its language, which I can well believe, for it's always a great comfort to the British when a foreigner is unable to use the Queen's English. And let us not underestimate our friend's importance to future generations; after the bomb drops—and drop it will, one of these days, if only by accident, or from the nature of things—the few miserable survivors will want to find some pride in the fact of their having been born to the race of men, and they'll go back —those of them that can read—to the poets and the writers to discover what men were like.

"And what will they find there, looking out at them from between the hard covers of his books? Badmeiler.

"Ah, the poor souls; it would take a Benét to write the full story of their astonishment."

Mr. Badmeiler, glass in hand, looked swimmingly at Miranda. "Hey there," he said uncertainly; "where've you been?"

She turned from him without speaking, and he gazed at us in owlish surprise. "She's been crying," he declared. "What's the matter, beautiful?"

Claude started toward him, and I put out my hand to stop him. "Take it easy," I said. "Nothing's the matter." I took the glass out of Badmeiler's hand and walked him to the door. "We've been putting the city to bed," I said.

I thought of Bee's last poem, from *Dreams and Sarabandes:*

So then to bed and bid the world goodnight.
Slow falls the moon across the western slopes.
See how the city in her lonely light
Puts out like lanterns one by one our hopes.

"Good night," I said to him. "You must come again some time."

CHAPTER 14

I DIDN'T see Miranda for a week or so; I thought
that perhaps she had gone away for a while, to the
shore or the desert. But one morning as I was sitting at my desk there was a knock on the door and
when I went to open it I found Abbie standing
there, big-eyed, staring up at me. "Can I talk to

you, Uncle Edward?" she asked. She looked a little thin, I thought. "Come in," I said. "What's on your mind?"

She sat down in the big chair, with her legs straight out in front of her, and regarded me solemnly. "What I want to know," she said at last, "is: can I come and live with you?"

I looked back at her just as solemnly, wondering what kind of game or grief or make-believe it was. "Of course," I said. "Certainly. When would you like to begin?"

"When Mommie leaves," she said simply; and a large tear slid quietly down her cheek.

No matter what I may have thought myself, or wondered or imagined, I wasn't ready to hear it from the child. I tried to sound amused, and hearty. "Well, well," I said; "what makes you think she's going to leave?"

"I heard them talking," said Abbie. "They thought I was asleep."

I could feel a little buzzer of alarm go off inside.

"To whom was she talking?" I asked as lightly as I could. "To Claude?"

"No," said Abbie. "It was somebody else. I couldn't hear him very well. She said 'Oh my darling,' and things like that. It wasn't Claude, because I'd have known if it was, and anyway, she never says 'Oh my darling' to him."

"Why do you think she means to leave?" I asked. "What gave you such an idea?"

"Because he kept saying that she had to," said Abbie. She gave a sudden dry small sob like a hiccup. "I don't care," she cried. "I don't care. She can go if she wants to."

Her little elfin face was frozen in desperate woe. "Who cares?" she said forlornly.

I went across and picked her up and set her on my lap. She stayed there like a little stone figure, unmoving, and without tears. "Your mother isn't going to leave you," I said. "Wherever she goes, you're going, too."

I hoped I was right; I had to believe it, and make Abbie believe it. But I wonder if even then

I knew what I believed. Whatever it was, there was no comfort in it—not for me, at any rate. Yet Abbie must have found some, because she seemed to relax a little, and her squablike body felt lighter and softer on my lap. She buried her head in my shoulder for a moment, and clung to me; then she raised her face and gave me a moth-soft kiss on the cheek. "Thank you, Uncle Edward," she said. "I guess maybe it'll be all right."

"Of course it will," I said. "Mothers always take their children with them when they go . . ." I hesitated. "On such a journey," I said.

"Then she *is* going!" breathed Abbie and clung to me again in sudden fright.

"I think so," I said slowly, committing myself at last.

"And me, too?"

I remembered that the woman Bee had loved had had a daughter. "Yes," I said; "you, too."

She took a deep breath and slid gravely off my lap to the floor. "I better go and pack my things," she said.

I walked with her to the door. "Good-bye, Uncle Edward," she said. "I'll send you a postcard."

It was the last time—but one—that I ever saw her.

The next day Claude approached me with a firm expression. "Miranda is dating someone else," he said.

I asked him how he knew, and if he knew who it was. "No, I don't," he said, "but she goes out and won't tell me where or with whom. I thought for a while it was this Badmeiler."

"That's scarcely likely," I said.

"Well," said Claude, "he does have something."

"What?" I asked.

"Fifty thousand dollars," said Claude bitterly.

"Oh, come!" I said. "That would never interest Miranda."

"No?" said Claude. "How can you be sure?"

"You can't," I said. I imagine that I sounded a little sharp. "You have to stop trying to be sure—

both for her and for yourself. She may want something much less . . . and much more."

"Yes, I know," he said mournfully: "fire and ice.
You told me." He gave a bleak, short laugh. "From
me?" he said.

"Anyway—it's probably too late now."

I thought it probably was, but I didn't tell him
so. "Have you ever really tried?" I asked. "Have
you ever really gone all out for anything?"

He thought about it for a while. "No," he said
at last, "I guess probably not. There's always a
thought somewhere in the back of my mind that
perhaps something else . . . well, how can you be
sure of anything? I know," he said quickly as
I started to interrupt, "I shouldn't say that; I
shouldn't always want to be sure of things. But
the trouble is, I do want to . . . if only of still
being alive the day after tomorrow. There are just
too many things now that can go wrong in the
world, there are too many things to think about,
things to worry about. . . ."

"Worry if you like," I said, "but if you give your heart, give all of it."

"All of it?" he said. "I thought I did. I mean . . . I meant to."

"Then try once more," I said.

"All right," he said. "Yes, I will." He took a long breath and stood up straight. "The best we had," he said, "was that one day at Chelly Canyon. It wasn't much, I guess it wasn't enough, but it was the best. Maybe I'll go back there and try again. Because it was the best."

I didn't have much hope for him; whatever magic was working on Miranda from the past was too strong, I thought. She was already committed. But for what it was, it was a gesture, and one that I knew he had to make.

He phoned me that night. "It's all arranged," he said. "We're going to the canyon tomorrow." He sounded excited and happy, and a little frightened. "Wish me luck, Uncle Edward," he said.

Miranda came by the next morning, to ask me to

keep an eye on Abbie while she was away. She had packed a box lunch for herself and Claude, and expected to be gone for most of the day, and had left peanut-butter sandwiches, a can of peaches, and a bottle of milk in the refrigerator for the children. "I told Abbie to ask Mortimer over," she said. "His mother will bring him, and if you'll just see that they get their lunch properly, and stay out of mischief. . . . Abbie can manage the lunch part of it, she's very good at it. I'll call for her myself when I'm ready, and take her out to supper somewhere; and Claude can drop Mortimer back home."

She came close to me and put her hand on my arm in a way she had and looked at me searchingly. "You've been very dear," she said; "thank you."

She leaned forward suddenly and kissed me. "That's for joy," she said.

She stopped at the door for a moment, and turned, and looked around at the room, as though she wanted to remember it. I thought that her eyes shone, as though there were tears in them, but it might have been the sunlight. She smiled at me and waved her hand, and then she was gone. I went out on the balcony and saw her get into Claude's car, and watched them drive away together. "Good luck," I said, but whether to Claude or to Miranda, I wasn't sure.

A little later Mortimer was brought over by his mother, and he and Abbie went down to the terrace to play. At noon I brought them in and gave them their lunch from the other apartment, and then they went downstairs again. I was busy looking over some old papers; the children's shrill, high voices fitted like bird sounds into the background.

It was when the voices stopped that I became aware of the silence. I waited a moment and heard nothing, and stepped out onto the balcony to see.

What I saw looked to me—at first—like a game: both children were motionless, frozen into attitudes of attention, as though they were waiting or listening for something. I saw Abbie hold up her hand, as though bidding Mortimer be quiet; I saw the boy's look of bewilderment; I thought that whatever it was she heard, she was the only one who heard it.

And then, suddenly, she gave a wild cry, and turned to Mortimer in a storm of tears. "I knew it, I knew it!" she cried. "We're going. Good-bye . . . good-bye, Mortimer; good-bye, everybody! Oh . . . good-bye!"

"Abbie!" I called. "What are you doing?" But she didn't hear me. Already she was running blindly down the street. "Wait!" she cried, "wait . . . I'm coming, too." Her little elfin body flitted and flickered in the bright noonday light, the criss-cross of cars coming and going threw shine and shadow over her, the trees hid her; only her voice came back to me, faint and desperate in the air:

"Wait for me, Mommie! Wait for me!"

By the time I got to the street, she had vanished.

CHAPTER 15

I TOOK Mortimer with me, and we got into my car and I backed it out of the garage under the apartment and started for the canyon. I couldn't think of anything else to do. If I was right, if Abbie was trying to reach her mother, I figured we'd pick her up in a few blocks; even a desperate child can't run very fast or very far. I had to get to Miranda; if Abbie was headed somewhere else, only Miranda would know where.

We didn't find her. Once or twice I saw a little girl running or walking down a street, but it wasn't Abbie. As we turned up Laurel toward the hills, a sheriff's car passed us, going very fast, its siren sounding and the red light flashing. I pulled over to let it go by; I didn't think it had anything to do with me.

But when we got to Chelly Canyon, the sheriff's car was there, and a police prowl car, and several people. They were spread out among the rocks and underbrush below the ledge; they seemed to be searching for something. Claude was with them; he was wet with perspiration, and he looked terrible. He came over to the car and got in and slumped down on the seat. "I didn't touch her," he said. "I wasn't anywhere near her."

I asked him what had happened.

He put his hand to his face and rubbed his eyes.

"Miranda went off the ledge," he said dully. "She fell, or something."

"Fell? . . . Off the ledge?"

He gestured helplessly. "I don't know," he said. "They can't find her. I saw her go. . . . We were talking, and I asked her to marry me. . . . We were just talking . . . and then she was gone. She was just gone. I can't find her, nobody can find her; she isn't there. The whole thing's crazy. . . . She has to be there, she went over, I saw her go. She fell, or something. I wasn't anywhere near her. I tell you, it's crazy."

A sheriff's deputy came striding over to us in his dust-brown uniform. "Are you sure there was someone up there with you, mister?" he asked Claude.

"Yes," said Claude desperately. "Yes."

"Well," said the officer, "the trouble is, we can't find where anybody could have fallen down this slope here. There's no signs of it, like anything was disturbed in any way. I mean, a body coming down here would break a few bushes, or the dirt would show some marks, wouldn't it? Maybe the lady just went home or something."

"That's probably it, officer," I said. "She probably just went home."

"You mean there aren't going to be any corpses?" asked Mortimer.

"That's right, son; no corpses," said the sheriff. "Not any."

"Oh, cow!" said Mortimer and lapsed into silence.

The sheriff went away, and Claude lay back against the seat and covered his eyes. "You believe me, Uncle Edward," he said, "don't you?"

I looked up at the empty ledge, and at the blue, wide, far-off sky above it. There didn't seem to be anything to say. Whatever had happened, it was done now, finally; wherever Miranda was, I had no doubt that Abbie was with her. They'd never find her body among the stones and boulders at the foot of the cliff.

"Yes, Claude," I said. "I believe you."

A new tenant has come to take Miranda's old apartment, a young woman by the name of Minnie McHugh. She has red hair and freckles, and is either a screen writer at Universal, or an actress at Paramount, or perhaps both, but we are not yet sufficiently acquainted for me to ask. I think that Claude finds her attractive; I don't blame him, I must admit that her saucy face and merry ways are very welcome in the neighborhood.

In my trunk of old letters and clippings there was one letter from Bee—his last. It had been a long time since I'd seen it, and I'd forgotten some of it. Now I took it out, to read again. It was from Zermatt, in the summer of '36; he wrote gaily, and spoke of his plans for the winter. "We are so happy," he wrote, "the three of us. Dear Edward, it is a most miraculous blessing to be together with the one you love—whom you have always loved, beyond time itself. The child is happy, too; we have bought her a little *klettering* outfit, and she talks so seriously to the guides, she wants to know how to do everything. There are two little boys here at the hotel who play with her; my darling calls them —heaven knows why!—Nifty Biddy and Nosey Robinson.

"Do you remember that you asked me once, 'What do the angels talk about?' and I said: 'Love and forever, without fear of change.' Well, it's true, that's what we talk about. We talk about how the sun comes up in the morning and shines on our faces, and how good the little croissants are with honey and sweet butter for breakfast. And how the nightingales sing forever on the other side of the mountains.

"We've taken a little chalet near Lauterbrunnen for later in the summer, and after Paris we'll probably go back to Florence in the spring, to Dolly Caracciolo's apartment near the park. After all, it was in Florence that I first knew . . . that we both first knew—

"Tomorrow we make an ascent on the Matterhorn—not to the top, not all the way. Just the two of us; it's still far beyond the child.

"I send you a few lines from one of your own sonnets—like rosemary for remembrance . . .

"*But to the lover beauty is his love,*
His heart's dear mistress ever at his side:
She is the blue bright wind of heaven above,
The light of evening on the valleys wide.
She is the sea . . .

"And so, good night, and love from all of us."

I put the letter down and took up my own book of poems and finished the sonnet for him. "She is the sea," I said aloud,

"*. . . she is the swifter tide*
Of narrower waters, and the forest green.
In all his courses beauty is his guide,
She goes before him, she is heard and seen,
And has a body. Let the lover tell
Whose voice he hears in music's sweetest part;
He knows the face of beauty, knows it well;

She is his friend, the treasure of his heart,
Which on the earth like benediction pours
A light he loves, a spirit he adores."

I touched the folded, yellowed newspaper clipping from the Paris *Herald*. I didn't need to open it. I knew so well what it said.

"Zermatt, June 15, 1936 . . ."

Books *by*

ROBERT NATHAN

NOVELS

The Color of Evening (1960)
So Love Returns (1958)
The Rancho of the Little Loves (1956)
Sir Henry (1955)
The Train in the Meadow (1953)
The Innocent Eve (1951)
The Married Look (1950)
The Adventures of Tapiola (1950)
(containing *Journey of Tapiola*, 1938, and
Tapiola's Brave Regiment, 1941)
The River Journey (1949)
Long after Summer (1948)
Mr. Whittle and the Morning Star (1947)
But Gently Day (1943)
The Sea-Gull Cry (1942)
They Went On Together (1941)
Portrait of Jennie (1940)
Winter in April (1938)
The Barly Fields (1938)
(containing *The Fiddler in Barly*, 1926,
The Woodcutter's House, 1927,

The Bishop's Wife, 1928,
The Orchid, 1931,
and *There Is Another Heaven,* 1929)
The Enchanted Voyage (1936)
Road of Ages (1935)
One More Spring (1933)
Jonah (1925)

POEMS
The Green Leaf (1950)
The Darkening Meadows (1945)
Morning in Iowa (1944)
Dunkirk (1941)
A Winter Tide (1940)
Selected Poems (1935)

THEATER
Jezebel's Husband & The Sleeping Beauty (1953)

NON-FICTION
Journal for Josephine (1943)

FOR YOUNG PEOPLE
The Snowflake and the Starfish (1959)

ARCHAEOLOGY
The Weans (1960)

These are BORZOI BOOKS, *published in New York
by* ALFRED A. KNOPF, INC.

A NOTE ABOUT THE AUTHOR

ROBERT NATHAN *was born in New York City in 1894, and was educated at private schools in the United States and Switzerland. While attending Harvard University he was an editor of the* Harvard Monthly, *in which his first stories and poems appeared.*

Except for two short periods during which he was a solicitor for a New York advertising firm and a teacher in the School of Journalism of New York University, Mr. Nathan has devoted his time exclusively to writing. He is the author of over forty volumes of poetry and prose, and from this body of distinguished work he has acquired a reputation as a master of satiric fantasy unique in American letters. He lives now in California with his wife, who was Miss Helen Shirley Kneeland of Salem, Massachusetts.

February 1961

A NOTE ON THE TYPE AND PRODUCTION

The text of this book is set in Caledonia, a Linotype face designed by W. A. Dwiggins (1880-1956), who was responsible for so much that is good in contemporary book design. Though much of his early work was in advertising and he was the author of the standard volume, Layout in Advertising, *Mr. Dwiggins later devoted his prolific talents to book typography and type design, and worked with great distinction in both fields. In addition to his designs for Caledonia, he created the Metro, Electra and Eldorado series of type faces, as well as a number of experimental cuttings that have never been issued commercially.*

This book was composed, printed, and bound by H. Wolff, New York. The paper was manufactured by P. H. Glatfelter Co., Spring Grove, Pa. Typography and binding based on designs by W. A. Dwiggins.

3 A